ERRORS, ENCOUNTERS AND ESCAPADES

T0129023

ERRORS, ENCOUNTERS AND ESCAPADES

Dimmon

ISBN: 978-1-4669-1047-8 (sc)
ISBN: 978-1-4669-1046-1 (e)

Trafford rev. 05/10/2012

www.trafford.com

North America & International
toll-free: 1 888 232 4444 (USA & Canada)
phone: 250 383 6864 ♦ fax: 812 355 4082

DEDICATED TO MY SISTER-COUSIN

DOLORES

"Chachi lived *HERE!*"

CHACHI was an American Indian boy who lived on a small ranch on the reservation, not too far from a small village called Cactus. Not far from Yuma. He lived with his Papa and his CHILD-Mama as he called her. He had no brothers or sisters.

He could ride a horse, shoot and kill a rabbit running full speed. He swam in the river that ran a few hundred feet behind his house. AND he wasn't afraid of OLD GREY COYOTE who lived farther out in the desert. He tried to avoid him, and HE tried to avoid Chachi.

Chachi's Papa owned a small herd of cattle. One of Chachi's chores was to milk their cow, Bella. He also helped feed them in the early morning and evening during the Fall and Winter months.

Another chore he had was to draw water from the well for washing the clothes and the dishes. But mostly Chachi pretended that he was a great Chief and his two dogs were his warriors, who fetched his game hens, rabbits and chased away his enemies. He roamed for a mile or so up and down the river.

It was not a big river at this point and Chachi could swim across it. He sometimes took his small rowboat out on his imaginary War Parties with his trusty warriors in tow. One day Chachi packed a lunch, took his two trusty warriors. He proceeded to walk south along the riverbank. He was enjoying his stroll on this superb blue-skyed, sunny morning. The Canine Warriors chased a few rabbits, squirrels and even scared some grouse from their nest in the grass and they went flying up in the air!

He had brought along his fishing pole so he sat down on the riverbank to fish. He caught three large enough to cook but he knew he wasn't to build a fire unless some adult was with him, so he put them in his knapsack. All at once as he walked along, he realized that he had come farther than he should have.

Trees were thicker here and the trail was becoming dimmer. The wind began to blow. He decided it was time for him to return home. But where Was home? The trees were very tall and dense. The sky had turned grey. He tried to remember where home was. He couldn't get his bearing by looking up at the sky—the sun was no longer there, only the grey cloudy sky. He began to get frightened! He decided the best thing to do was to stay near the river, so he listened for its sound. He thought he heard it over on the right side, so he walked that direction. He had walked for some time, but he didn't find the river. He stopped and listened again. He could hear the water moving but he couldn't tell exactly where it was. The sky was getting darker and Chachi knew it was going to rain. He knew that if it rained *too* much, the river would overflow its banks and flood the area. Just then a roll of thunder sounded and a bright flash of lightening lit up the sky. It began to rain so hard that he could barely see where he was going within a half hour he knew the river would flood. He must find some kind of shelter. He walked farther, looking for any kind of shelter. The lightening had almost stopped but the rain kept pouring down from the dark sky. SUDDENLY, he saw something he could use for shelter! A large almost—dead trees with an opening in the trunk large enough for him to crawl into. It was at least out of the rain! He felt very tired and his eyes wanted to close—and they did.

His eyes flew open when he felt the water creeping into the hollow of the tree. Chachi knew he must get higher. As he stood up he saw that maybe he could possibly climb higher. It was a tall tree and if he could climb high enough the water might not reach him. He knew these storms passed in an hour or two. So up, up climbed Chachi until he found a spot where he could sit. He put his bottom against the small ledge and tested it. It appeared to hold his weight. Again he fell asleep. This time when he awoke the sun was shining and the water had receded some. He could see that if he climbed down he would have to wade water to exit the tree. He climbed down and out of the tree.

Now that the storm had passed, he could hear the river rushing by and knew by the sound of it, that he could not get too close. But could follow its sound by walking farther from the river where he was now. He soon came to the place where his Papa kept the Yearlings. They were standing inside their shed. He knew that he was near home, and he began to run. As he burst in the door his Mama asked where he'd been—out so early. Go change your clothes and come eat your breakfast. He Couldn't Believe That His Mother Hadn't Missed HIS absence!! His father must be out feeding the cows and waiting for Chachi to finish his breakfast so he can milk the cow. Chachi smiled to himself and shook his head. What kind of parents did he have?

After this, Chachi decided to be more careful on his next adventure, since no one noticed if he was gone. Maybe he wouldn't be missed at all. He'd have to manage on his own. He *must* continue to *learn* things.

The next week Papa told him they would be going into town for supplies. Chachi loved their trips for supplies! He got to play with the local children in the schoolyard. School was closed for the summer. The town's Children met there for their recreation. Chachi had met a special boy there last summer and they had become friends. They played marbles, baseball and shot their bows in an empty lot behind the Church.

On these trips to town his Mama bought materials for her dresses and shirts for Chachi and Papa. They were in town all day on Supply Day. His Papa talked to the men as they played their games of dominoes in the Parlor behind the feed store. Chachi and Mama loaded the supplies in Papa's old truck. When this was finished they had supper in a small cafe that served Mexican food. Chachi LOVED tacos best! They even had a ice cold drink; an orange or strawberry soda?

There was a refrigerator at Chachi's house but it was old and it didn't get the sodas icy-cold like the ones from the Mexican Cafe. They also had a new cook stove that used propane. Mama said it cooked so much better than the wood burning stove. She had been so happy when his Papa had brought it home and took the other one back to be sold again.

About six miles along the river from where Chachi lived was a family named Maderios. They had been friends with his parents for many years. They had a son named Ruben who was Chachi's BEST friend. Ruben had two sisters; Angelina and Rachel. They visited each other two or three times a year. Chachi and his parents had spent Christmas at their house a few times and they had spent a few Thanksgivings at Chachi' parents. They always spent NEW YEAR together at one place or the other.

One day in June's lovely blue-sky and Fluffy Cloud day, Chachi told his mom he was taking his boat and going to visit with Ruben. I'll be home before dark, he said. Chachi packed some snacks in his knapsack, took his rifle and his two Canine Commandos and off they rode into adventure! The river was smooth and clear. There were no rapids or falls A few rocks but nothing major between his house and the Maderios place to fear. The dogs lay quietly sleeping as Chachi rowed along. He had gone about two and a half miles when he began to set a HAIR-ON-END chill-down-the spine-feeling. He looked very casually on both sides, but he saw nothing and his dogs were quiet. He rowed slowly on. Then he saw the place where the river narrowed because of a few small rocks he must pass. He thought he saw movement on the right bank. He glanced again but was busy maneuvering the boat and when he looked again, he saw nothing. He drew in his oars and floated for a minute or two while he scanned the river on both sides for any movement, but saw nothing. He dipped his oars in the water again as they neared the area where the river's bank were higher on both sides. At This moment he saw someone dive into the river, a man with big bushy black eyebrows and whiskers with a broad face. The man grabbed the boat and both dogs went into action, but the man had a gun and he shot at them as they started to attack him. The big man turned the boat over spilling the dogs and Chachi. The dogs were swimming for the shore one, bloody from a shot and the man was searching for Chachi, *but*—Chachi was already near the shore. As soon as the boat rolled over, Chachi dived under and began to swim toward an area where cattails grew. Chachi knew if he could reach it, there was a trail hidden from view of the river by the indented riverbank. If he could reach the thickly wooded bank area! He swam as fast as he could! He knew that he would have to come up for a breath soon and just when he thought he could hold his breath no longer, he saw the roots of the cattails and slowly eased his head up and took in air. He could see the big man going for the shore in the area where the dogs exited the river. He wasn't at the shore yet. Chachi took the trail from the cattails up to the top of the bank and crawled quickly into the trees. He could see the big man almost to the shore. Chachi ran! He knew that his dogs had hightailed it home. *IF* his papa Or Mama saw the wound his Papa would come looking for him. *IF THEY saw* the wound!

He ran until his side began to ache and he slowed his step. He looked behind him but could see no one or hear anything. He must keep going on to the Maderios' although now he was on the opposite side of the river. He had been running for about ten minutes since he left the cattails and still saw no one or heard anything. He was contemplating a small rest when there, through the trees, he saw HIM. He was looking straight ahead and panting loudly. Chachi dropped fast to the ground and breathed softly. The big man's footsteps halted and Chachi knew he was looking all round. Finally Chachi heard him running again.

Chachi got slowly to his feet and began to run in the opposite direction, back toward his home. As he got to the place where the cattails grew—there was his boat in the cattails but where were the oars? He wanted to take his boat, but he had no oars so he left it there caught in the cattails. As he was running along there, where his dogs had exited the river lay his oars! The Great Spirit was watching over Chachi today! He looked and listened carefully and intently but he heard nothing. He quickly took his oars back to the boat, freed it and rowed on home.

The dogs, both of them were under the porch, Chachi went inside. His Mama was busy making bread. She smiled at him and asked if he'd has a good time? Chachi told her that his boat had turned over in the river and that the dogs had run away. That he had righted it and come back home. She told him he was a brave boy then said "Come have your lunch." Chachi was beginning to realize WHY the Great Spirit chose to give only one child to his Mama—She was a child herself!

Chachi heard a week or so later that the man who had attacked him was arrested for stealing a horse over in the village.

Chachi never mentioned this incident to his Papa.

Chachi was seventeen today! His Papa had been raising cattle since Chachi was a little boy, and it had paid off. His cattle were some of the best around! Men came out to his place to purchase some of them each Spring All his yearlings became sires and sold for hundreds of dollars each. Chachi had helped Papa for the last four or five years to achieve this position in the cattle raising business. His parents now had a new big house and barn. There were many more cows now, a large herd and, of course, yearlings out in their pasture.

Chachi was a tall boy now. About 5 feet and 10 inches and he weighed about ONE HUNDRED and sixty pounds. His Papa had purchased horses a few years back, as the herd enlarged, for Chachi and himself. Chachi still had his boat, but one of his canine warriors had died of old age about a year ago and the other one didn't get around much because of arthritis in the hips. He would go soon and the thought of it made Chachi sad.

Chachi was off to college this year to study Business Law. He would use this in the future to help his Papa in the cattle business. The ranch would belong to Chachi someday, but until then, it was Papa's *and* his ranch.

Chachi came home to the ranch each Summer when the term was over. He loved the ranch! He always had. He helped with the cattle all Summer. He helped from the birthing to the final sales. He sometimes got a little sad to see some of them go, but the money was being applied (deposited) to the ranch's account, and this made the family happy.

Chachi still loved adventure so each Summer found him out along the river in his boat fishing or hunting. He never ventured farther away in the wooded area of the property. OLD GREY Coyote was still alive but was old now, not enough pep left in him to do any running. If Chachi came upon him, he would turn to face Chachi and give one of his most vicious snarls, teeth, (what he had left) bared, Chachi never had the heart to shoot him. He would stand very still until OLD GREY COYOTE turned and walked away. Chachi admired the Old Grey Coyote, his former enemy, for his bravery in the face of danger.

One day while out horseback riding, Chachi came across horse tracks around the fence of the yearlings pasture. He got off his horse to look closely at them. They weren't his or his Papa's track—they had their horseshoes made over in Yuma. He knew that their shoes had a star in the center on each side. These were a lazy J show prints. Why were they here so near the fence of the yearlings pasture? There were two different sets of prints.

One was the lazy J and one had a rocking *M*. So who was trespassing? Chachi followed the prints to the river's edge. They crossed here and he rode his horse thru to the other side. Yes, they had come out here. He followed them for a mile or so until the tracks disappeared in the rocky ground. Chachi turned around when he heard someone ride up. "You're on private land her," said an older man with a thick black, bushy beard and bushy eyebrows. "What are you looking for?"

"Nothing in particular," answered Chachi, "just out for a ride. I live across the river on the TWIN STAR ranch. How long have you owned this land on this side of the river? It's Indian Land, part of the reservation."

The bearded man spat tobacco juice and looked into Chachi's eyes and gave a ruthless laugh. "Oh, I rented it from the reservation office over in Yuma. I'm on it legally. Why do you ask?"

"Well, our ranch across the river is *Definately Ours*, legally and I hope you remember, *As I Will*, which side _we_ belong on. And with this said, Chachi turned and rode back across the river. That man somehow looked familiar. Where had Chachi seen him before? It was later when Chachi was in bed almost asleep when suddenly his eyes flew open. Now I know where I've seen him—that's the man who jumped in the river and turned my boat over when I was younger and on my way to Ruben's house. Who was he?

The next morning at breakfast Chachi told his Papa about the man who was living a few miles down the river on the opposite side and told him about finding the tracks which was why, he, was crossing the river. He had followed tracks that he had found near the yearlings fence, over to the other side until he came to the rocky ground. This same man tried to steal my boat and chased me for a mile before I lost him. This was when I was eleven on my way to Ruben's. This is the same man. He didn't recognize me but I recognized him, Papa. "We'd better take the new dog down there at night for awhile," said Papa.

Chachi had been courting Angelina for the last year. He thought she was beautiful with her green eyes and dark hair. He loved her sense of humor and her tomboyish ways. She could ride a horse almost as well as he, could rope cattle or horses and he'd never want to compete with her in a shooting contest! for fear he would lose, yet she was a lady, his lady. She could dance like no one else he had ever known. He was taking her dancing tonight at the Center. There would be food to eat and sodas to drink. Ruben had a girlfriend who lived in the little village of Cactus which was about three miles past the Maderios place. Her name was Celia. They had known each other most of their lives. They ALL had gone to school together there in Cactus.

The Maderios' raised grapes. Their vineyard wasn't a large one and they sold their grapes to the small wineries, which sold THEIR wines along the river to towns and villages for a distance of seventy miles in both directions. The Maderios' were well known and well liked.

They left about eight p.m., He, Angelina and Ruben. Celia was meeting them at the Center. She was waiting dressed in her full skirt and sandals, ready to dance! She smiled as they came to where she sat. Her hair hung loose around her shoulders. Angelina had worn a

Sun Dress which also had a full skirt and she, too, wore sandals. Her hair was braided up around her head with flowers woven among the braids. Both girls looked beautiful.

The music started at nine O'clock and would go on until Twelve Midnight. The band consisted of; Two guitars, a lead and a base, an accordion, a violin, a trumpet and a base Fiddle. The bank took a break about Ten O'clock for a cold drink and a Taco or Burrito, then back to the music and dancing!

Chachi loved how wonderful it felt to hold Angelina in his arms for the slow dances. He could feel her heart beating against his chest. He wanted to pick her up in his arms and Wisk her away to some Magical Place and make her his. He caught himself breathing hard and Angelina asked if he wanted to sit for awhile? He decided very quickly that sitting was a good idea before he made a complete ASS of himself! They all sat at one of the tables and had another cold, icy drink. His eyes told Angelina how he felt about her and she knew that she must be careful. For she herself felt some of these feelings for Chachi.

She was sure that she and Chachi were expected to wed someday, but her Father said she must wait to be married for another two years. Chachi would be finished with his schooling, them she would see how she felt. Ruben and Celia joined them at this point for another cold drink, too. About Eleven-thirty they were ready to go. Everyone's feet were tired and achy. The moon was big and bright as they drove along and the moon held Magic in its glow. Chachi held Angelina against his side as he drove. Her nearness and the moonlight took his breath away! Ruben and Celia were moaning in the backseat—this was too much for Chachi so he pulled to the side of the road and stopped. He took Angelina into his arms which turned him ON. He wanted more than she was willing to give, so he started the car and drove THEM all home. When he parked his car in his yard, he knew that he wouldn't sleep so he walked along the river and that's how he found the bearded man and his friend on Chachi's side of the river on hi s property. He surprised them and they reined in their horses fast.

"Hey—did you forget which side of the river is yours?" asked Chachi. "I thought we had settled that already. Do you have an explanation for me?"

"AS a matter of fact, I do; We were over on our side, when we saw two riders crossing to your side, so we followed them to make sure they weren't crossing to your place.

We thought we'd better make sure they weren't here looking over your herd of young Bulls.

"And," ask Chachi, "Were they over at my herd's pasture?"

"No, the big man answered, they rode off in the opposite direction along the river. We're on our way back now, Goodnight." Chachi decided to go check on the herd anyway. They seemed to be fine and most were sleeping. A few stirred and Mooed when he walked up. They were fine. He was turning to go on home when he noticed fresh horse droppings and decided to see if there were any hoof prints. Yes, there they were, a set of lazy J and the *M*. So they had been here. He'd better warn Papa of this discovery. They might have to post a guard tomorrow night. The next morning he told Papa about the men and the hoof prints around the bulls pasture. Papa posted men for a few nights, but nothing happened. The men were not so fond of just one man guarding all night long, so two men took shifts. One guarded from eight to twelve and then the other took the twelve to eight shift. On the third night the cattle dog started snarling and the hair bristled up on his back. Seth who was on duty, awoke Troy and both were awake, alert with their rifles ready. They could hear noises closer along the river, but no one came near the corral. They heard the riders pass by and Seth called out "Who goes there?" but not a word was aid. They were heard crossing the river. In the morning Seth and Troy searched along the river crossing and sure enough, one lazy J and the *M*. They reported this to Chachi's Papa, who in turn told Chachi.

The next night found Chachi camped near the river-crossing about 300 feet in the direction of the bulls pasture in the trees nearer the river. His rifle was loaded and laying near his hand. About Twelve-Thirty P.M., he heard the hooves of the horses moving very quietly and slowly coming across the river. He heard them enter the river walking their horses quietly. They mounted and rode up on Chachi's side. They stopped and conversed in whispers. They began to move toward the bulls corral. Chachi very quietly picked up his rifle and crept up to the corral. He was standing beside one of the fence post, rifle pointing and quietly said "Drop those wire cutters and your guns—Now! They were so surprised and at that moment Chachi said "I wouldn't *Even Think* about *Running*, you make a big target, Slim." Chet chose this moment to speak, "Don't Shoot, this wasn't my idea!" and that was when Slim knocked him from his horse, and turned and made a dash for the river. That's when the rifle rang out with a shot and slim fell from his horse. Chachi walked up to him and said "Crawl back to the corral," where Chet sat mutely. Chachi took his long leather thongs and tied Slim up first and then Chet. He tied their ankles next. Then he tied their feet to their hands, behind them. He got on his horse, said "Goodnight boys" the sheriff will be out in the morning to pick you up." Then Chachi turned and whistled for the guard dog. "Sit and guard" said Chachi. The dog sat, gave a snarl and lay down flat on its stomach, his eyes on the men. Chachi took their two horses by their reins and led them to the house, where he put them in the barn.

In the morning the Sheriff came out, saw the wire cutters, and looked at the hoof-prints and saw that they were made from the shoes that their horses wore. He packed them off to jail where he found that Slim was on the property illegally and was wanted for a murder done during one of his robberies, so Slim was sent away for LONG time and, Chet as an accessory to the robbery was given eighteen to thirty years.

When Chachi was twenty-two, he was finished with his schooling completely. He was still at home helping his Papa with the ranch. Papa had hired two Hands to help him while Chachi finished his schooling. One of them was the Ranch's Brander for the cattle. He was two years younger than Chachi and his name was Cameron. He had lived on a ranch all his life. In fact, he was the Brander there. The ranch had belonged to his uncle, and when the uncle died it was sold. The uncle had left Cameron's mother some money so she had bought herself a small place and Cameron had moved on. He and Chachi became friends. Soon he was dating Rachel, Angelina's sister. They rode together to pick up the girls for picnics to fish from the boat, and, of course, for the Dances! Cameron Loved to dance. They all enjoyed each other's company.

One day Papa said to Chachi "Are you ready for your own Spread now?" I imagine you're about ready to ask Mr. Maderios for Angelina's hand in Marriage, aren't you? Our Herd Is large enough to split in half, now or you take as many as you want. How about that Nice Old ANGELO Spread across the river and down about two miles?" It was a nice place. "Have you been there lately?"

"Well, Papa, I see you've been thinking about this, and No, I haven't been by the ANGELO place since I came back from college, is it for sale?"

"I head when I was in town a few weeks ago that MR. ANGELO died while on a trip to Mexico, unexpectedly—heart Attack. Mrs. Angelo went to live with her son in Phoenix and that the place was for sale. "This might be a good time to go have a look around, don't you think so?"

Why, yes, Papa, I do! I think I'll go right on over now and have a look. He waved and rode off. He crossed the river at the usual place. As he came out of the water and up the bank he could see the place where Slim once lived. It was a small house but it sat on a beautiful spot of ground. It was top center of a small knoll. There was a big Oak tree in the yard and there were roses. Surely these weren't planted by Slim!! As he came nearer, a woman walked out onto the porch with a rifle in her hand. He was too far away to see her face but he waved and said "I live on the Double Star Ranch across the river, I'm just passing through. Did you just move here?" She motioned for him to come forward, which he did and stopped at the edge of the yard.

"Yes, she said, we move din about two weeks ago. Actually, Mom and I came on out and father and the Men are bringing the cattle. We are expecting them any day. We don't have a large herd, just enough to get by with. We sell the milk and butter from the cows and we sell the males for beef. We keep one or two to butcher for ourselves, tho. I understand you have a large Spread and top of the market cattle" she smiled.

"It's my Papa's spread, but he thinks it's time for me to get my own spread and cattle, so I'm on my way to the old ANGELO place a little farther down the river," he said.

"Oh! so you and your wife will be our neighbor?" she said.

"Well, I have no wife—yet, but we, Papa and I, may buy it anyway. I think Papa's ready for a smaller herd right now, less work. He thinks it's time for me to find a wife," he smiled embarrassed.

"And is it? time I mean, for a wife Or do you already have someone chosen?"

"Actually—No—Not Really. I've been going with one of the Maderios daughter's, Angelina. But she has other friends she goes out with, too. We've ALL been friends most of our lives. She has a brother who has been My best friend since we were six years old. His name is Ruben. They have another sister named Rachel who dates our Brander, Cameron."

"Good she said, my name is Victoria Ingels, and my friends call me Tory. I'm not spoken for yet, so maybe we can be friends, too."

"I would like that fine," said Chachi, and now I must be on my way. OH! MY name is CHACHI," and he rode on to see his future home—perhaps?" Quite a friendly girl he thought and Very beautiful! She has hair like spun gold and eyes the color of the sky. She was truly splendid!

Chachi rode on to look at the Old Angelo place. He rounded a bend and there it sat. The house was large with a long front porch. He could see the well from where he sat. Then he rode on to the back to look at the barn. It was in good shape. A big barn with a hayloft. He dismounted and opened the door to look inside. He climbed the ladder to look at the hayloft. It all appeared to be sturdy. He stepped upon the porch to have a peek through the window. The living room was wonderfully long with a fireplace on the central middle wall the wall between the living room and the bedrooms next to it. This was the East wall of the living room. In the west wall there were two big windows. Next, he stepped upon the smaller back porch and peeped into the kitchen. The refrigerator and the stove were placed on the west wall with cabinets and cupboards. On the east end, thru a wide archway was the dining room. He was pleased with the house and the barn. Yes, he was sure he could live here happily—especially with such a lovely lady for a neighbor.

He reported to his Papa later that he would be pleased to own the old Angelo Place. It was still in good shape and he liked it, but he wasn't quite ready for a wife—yet. He then told his Papa about the girl with the Golden hair and astounding blue eyes! Papa smiled at Chachi and said, "I've never known a woman with gold hair and blue yes, *but*, I'm sure if I *were YOU*, I'd ask the *Great Spirit* to help you with this one. Chachi," and he smiled.

The next week they purchased The Angelo Place for Chachi. He would move in after he had the cobwebs gone and the spiders chased away, his well pump serviced and his propane tank filled. This would take the biggest part of a week, he thought, but his Mama asked him if he could take his bedroom furniture on over to his house, so she could set up his room as a sewing room for herself. She already had her machine sitting at the door. Because she was his Child-Mama he took his things to his place and put them in what would be his guest room. He loved his Mama.

Chachi decided that he would paint the living room and the kitchen. He chose a sand beige for the living room and a buttercup yellow for the kitchen. He began on Monday of the following week. He had painted two walls of his kitchen, when he heard a knock on his door. He went, paint brush in hand, to answer it. He opened the door and there stood Tory, with her paint brush, she said "I've come to help you, neighbor, if I may."

"Of course you may," answered Chachi. "I always appreciate help—and from a Beautiful lady—I'd be a fool to say No, come on in" and he held the door open for her.

"What a nice big house," said Tory, "do you like it?"

"Yes, I truthfully do. I've always like this place. I came when I was younger to milk the cow for Mrs. Angelo, who had a crippled hand, when Mr. Angelo was gone on his buying trips. They had no children living here then."

"What a nice thing to do," said Tory, "Was she a nice lady?"

"Yes, a very nice lady. She treated me very well. I think she missed not having children, tho," said Chachi.

"I'm an only child, myself," said Tory, "so I plan on having a houseful! It's lonely being an only child."

"Well, I certainly can relate to that, I'm an only child, too I always wanted a brother. I, too, plan to have many children." Chachi stated emphatically!

"Where shall I start painting," Tory asked? "How about if I start on the wall next to the living room and we'll meet in the middle of the West wall, will that be okay?"

"Great idea," answered Chachi, "since I'm almost finished with the back wall.

They began to paint and had been doing so for a few minutes when Tory suddenly said, "You told me that you have a girl you date—daughter of another of our neighbors, is she a Special girl or just a friend?

He thought for a minute and answered, "She's definitely a Special friend. I'm not IN love with her, but I love her. We've known each other for many years. Her brother, Ruben has been my best friend since we were six. Our families are close friends, *but* we're not a Couple or engaged. She goes out with other friends of ours. We've never discussed marriage as neither of us are ready for that yet," he explained.

"I'm glad," she said, as she smiled at him with those big, blue yes. He looked at her and smiled back. Yes, he thought this is my kind of woman! He knew! He didn't know *HOW* he knew, *but* he knew!

When they began to paint the west wall they worked quietly. He started on the South end and she began on the north end. They met in the middle. WoW, it looks great, he said, "Thanks a lot!" Without realizing it he leaned over and kissed her on the cheek. She glanced up at him and said, "You're welcome, thank you for allowing me to help you." He realized that a man could get lost in eyes like that!

"When are you going to Officially move in—start living here," she asked?

"About the middle of next week, I imagine. I'll be picking up some of my furniture then, so I should be living here by the end of the week. I have to do some fence mending before I bring my cattle here. I'm starting with a small herd as I'll be doing most of the work myself. Speaking of cattle, did your dad get here with your cows yet?"

"Yes, they got here day before yesterday and everything went well. Dad has to build a barn, a small one, for the birthing and for Winter's cold weather, and, of course, for the milking. He's already hired a crew to begin building. I'm sure you'll hear the noise. Mama already has people for her milk and butter sales."

"That's good," he said. "I'm glad she has customers already lined up for her sales."

"I guess we're ready to go now," said Chachi. "Thanks Again. Maybe I'll see you on Wednesday when I bring the furniture." He closed and locked his front door. He took the reins of his horse and walked beside Tory to her place. He then mounted his horse and rode back to Papa's. His Mama asked if he had made himself something to eat and IF his stove worked good? He just smiled at her and said everything was fine. His Child-Mama didn't remember that the propane to Run the stove wouldn't be delivered until Wednesday. Mama was still a little girl, but he loved her.

Chachi went to the store that afternoon and ordered his furniture, good sturdy furniture. He bought a sofa, two chairs, a coffee table, a bookcase, a game table with two chairs, for his living room. For the kitchen he bought; an oak table with four chairs and a small hutch for the wall that Tory had painted. He bought pots and pans, dishes and drinking glasses, silverware, a broom, a mop, and a stopper for his sink! For his bedroom, he bought a big oak bed and dresser, a chest of drawers and mattress and box spring. He bought linens and towels and a shower curtain. Some of the smaller things he brought home in the truck and the furniture would be delivered from the Store on Wednesday. He was very tired that evening but he did play a game of checkers with Papa who beat him and tried not to smile too broadly so as not to anger Chachi! Papa said they would wait until Chachi was all settled in before they move his herd to his place. He hugged Papa goodnight and went to sleep out on the side porch on the couch, SINCE he had already took his old bedroom furniture over to his house, *SO MAMA* could *use* that room for her *Sewing Room*! Bless his Child-Mama. He sometimes felt sorry for her.

He dreamed of an angel with blond hair and blue eyes, cooking breakfast in his newly painted kitchen. She wore a big apron and nothing else! It was a good dream!

Today was Wednesday and his furniture would be arriving soon. He quickly got dressed, saddled his horse and rode to HIS HOUSE!

He had been there for about an hour and was busy putting up his new screens for the windows, when he saw his neighbor Miss Tory on her way to his house with a large basket on her arm. He watched her walking and was reminded of a beautiful palomino pony—lively and frisky.

"Hello and good morning," she said, "I see you are already at work."

"Yes, I've been here since early this morning. Slept over at Papa's on a couch on the side porch," He said, "because Mama has already changed my room into her Sewing Room! So it was the enclosed porch for me."

"Speaking of sewing, said Tory, I made a few sets of curtains for you, *IF* you like them, BUT *IF* you don't, please feel free to say so. My Mama told me I should have asked you first, that I might offend you by not asking first. I'm ready for the scolding, Chachi."

"Well, maybe I'd better see them first before the scolding, I will need curtains. Shall we go in and see if I need to give you a good scolding!"

The ones for the kitchen and dining room were of a white background with small tiny yellow flowers with a blue dot center. They made the rooms look so fresh and Finished.

The next room for curtains were the guest room where his old bedroom furniture was. Tory chose a plaid for this room, in mulberry, blue and green. They were perfect for the blue cover that he had on his bed. "It looks just perfect for this room," said Chachi to Tory. "You did a good job. You are a good seamstress, do *you* have a *sewing room?*"

"Oh, No," answered Tory, you've seen how small our house is, my machine is in my bedroom."

Next they went into Chachi's bedroom. His furniture wasn't there yet but the bedcover was laying on his old trunk. It was a soft green color. She had made wide striped curtains of green, tan, burgundy and yellow. She even made two pillows to sit on top of his trunk. The curtains brightened his room beautifully.

Chachi turned and gave Tory a kiss on the cheek, saying "Thank you so much, Tory and tell your mother that I like all of them, so there was no scolding, only thanks. Someone's going to be lucky to get you for a wife—you sew, cook and you are a good painter, too."

And added Tory, "I milk cows, make butter, cut firewood, plant and care for my garden of flowers and vegetables,—so if you run into any of your friends who need a good wife, you Might want to mention me" and she gave him a big teasing smile. This thought somehow made Chachi's heart beat fast and say to himself—No, I want you for myself. this surprised him and for a minute he thought he had said this out loud.

"Don't look so shocked, Chachi, I was only teasing you. I'm not ready for being a wife yet and I wouldn't know which of your friends to choose—I don't even know your friends." I must be going now and help Mama with the butter making. I'll see you later, Chachi" and she started to go home. After a few steps she turned, smiled at him and said, "I think I'd choose you from among all your friends, none could be nicer than you" and she threw him a kiss, turned and walked home. He watched her all the way until the bend in the road his her from his view. OH! Yes! You are So right Papa, I need help from The Great Spirit with this one. She is ALL Woman, Papa!

The end of September a dance was scheduled over in the Village at the Center. Chachi knew that Angelina would be expecting him to take her. He Really Wasn't in the mood, but Angelina would expect it.

He and Cameron took the car to pick up the girls. The music was fine, the cold drink was fine, but HE wasn't fine! Angelina was quietly watching him all evening and finally she said "I need to talk to you, Chachi. I know that you and I have been friends for a long time and our parents'

Her family had been asking her to tell me and tonight, she did.

"And how do you feel about it" Tory asked?"

"Absolutely Wonderful!!" Chachi answered. Angelina and I will *always* be friends but it's not in the stars for us to be married. She loves someone else and I hope to find my love, too, so we are both happy."

"Then I'm glad for you Chachi, and I hope you find her soon. You need her to tend and care for your house, and eventually your children all those children you said you wanted—remember?" Tory laughed.

"Hey, look, the moon has come up. So you want to take a walk?" He asked Tory.

"Sure," she said, "but let me tell my parents first." She went inside and came back with a shawl over her shoulders. "In case the wind decides to blow," she said.

"Let's walk along the river and I'll show you an old house that is said to be haunted. It's about a mile or so past my place."

"Ok," answered Tory, "I've never seen a REAL HAUNTED house. Have you ever seen anything there?" asked Tory.

"Well, to tell you the truth, I don't believe in Ghosts. I had an old, great, grandfather when I was four and I remember him talking about ghosts, but I've never seen any," said Chachi. Are you afraid?"

"ME?" asked Tory. "Of course not! but I will ask you to stay near me and hold my hand just in case!" and with this said, she reached for his hand. His blood began to pound and his heart began to race.

They had been walking for about ten minutes when they came to a most heavenly spot. It was green like a well-kept lawn. A few wild flowers grew in spots and an old grey log lay along one side, as if it had been placed there for seating. They sat down and Tory spoke softly "Do you suppose this is where they have their meetings?"

"What meetings?" asked Chachi.

"OH, the Ghosts perhaps or the Elves, the Fairies—The Ancients," said Tory.

"Well, to be perfectly honest, It was a meeting place for my Ancestors long ago. They sometimes came here to call on THE GREAT SPIRIT."

"So," said Tory, We may be on Holy Ground. We must show respect. Shall we say a silent prayer?"

"Let's do that," said Chachi. And they both bowed their heads and said their own thing to THE HOLY SPIRIT. Then they walked on holding hands.

They came through a small copse of trees and there it stood! An Old, OLD house with vegetation growing upon each side, windows were gaping holes. The old porch was sagging in the middle and the steps up to the porch were gone or broken. It had a tall chimney and amazing as it was stood tall! There was an old barn behind and to the left with hay from years ago up in the hayloft. It could be seen from where they stood in the front yard. The trees were full of moss hanging from like torn and tattered lace of an old ancient wedding dress.

"It's rather sad than scary, isn't it Chachi? Imagine—It was once a Splendid place where people lived, loved, children were born—probably buried here someplace. I wouldn't be surprised IF it does have ghosts. If I'd been born here, lived her happily with my Love and my children—I'd come back once-in-a-while to visit," said Tory in a sad voice.

"Well let's start back," said Chachi—I don't want your parents to worry about you being late. So they just enjoyed the walk, the moon and each other.

When they got to Tory's porch she thanked him for the moonlit walk, the Fairy Circle and the Old Haunted House. Then she said "This has been a Magical night, I don't know if it's the moon, the walk, the old Haunted House—or You, Chachi, but it's been one of my favorites. Thank You again." She looked up with those blue eyes and he took her in his arms and kissed her soundly! "Goodnight," he said, as he walked away to his house. He was too excited to sleep or just sit so he took out his cards and played a game of solitaire Until his eyes began to droop. He fell asleep thinking of how wonderful Tory felt in his arms, wondering what was his next step? He loved his house and was glad he had bought it. It did look quite differently with its newly painted walls and those curtains.

The following week was spent putting a corral and fencing for his cattle. He made a fenced pasture for his yearlings. He was very tired when the evening came! He went to bed early and arose early. When the second week came to an end, he had a fenced pastureland for his herd of cattle. He would talk to Papa tomorrow, Saturday and see if Papa wanted to do the move the following weekend. Cameron would help with the short drive to Chachi's place. He would also do the branding of the yearlings. Papa's brand was two stars side by side. He asked Chachi if he wanted a completely different brand OR would he want the same two stars BUT with a rocker underneath them? If Chachi wanted the rocking stars for his brand. It would save a lot of time on the branding, since the cattle already had the twin stars, Cameron would only have to put the rocker under the stars. Chachi agreed to the rocking stars for his brand. Papa decided to brand them before the drive to Chachi's place.

Chachi's pastureland had some oak trees which was shade for the cattle in the hot summer days. Since his land was nearer the river than Papa's, his pastureland was greener. This meant less feed to buy during the winter months. On the other hand Chachi had to do double-post fencing as he knew how the river could rise and flood its banks. This meant that the yearling pasture, corral, and shed had to be farther inland. Actually his place was quite a bit higher than Papa's. This was because the riverbank on the East side was higher than its West bank. Wise Mr. Angelo had built his house on one of the highest points of land on the East side of the river. His Papa's land was lower on the West side, but farther away from the river.

Chachi had a free Saturday and wanted to take Tory dancing—but NOT to the Center! He wanted to take her into Yuma to a dinner and dancing. About ten in the morning he knocked on her door. She answered. She asked him to come in but he told her he had some work to do. He told her he had come to ask her, if she would go to dinner and dancing, with him tonight, over in Yuma?

She answered, "OH! I'd love that ever so much, Chachi" as she gave him a hug. He was a little embarrassed with Tory's mother but she smiled and said, "Good morning, Chachi." He answered with a "good morning to you." He then told Tory he would pick her up about seven thirty that evening.

He was there at exactly seven-thirty all decked out in his new Wranglers, A western Levi type shirt and his newest pair of cowboy western boots. As he was about to knock on the door it was opened by Tory. Tory was in a blue halter dress, her hair up with red high-heels. There was an embroidered red flower on the bodice of her dress. "I'm ready," she said, "bye, Mom," and she wrapped a red scarf around her shoulders. "I'll see you both when I get back" and she hugged both of them. She took Chachi's arm and they walked to the car.

They arrived about eight-forty P.M. They found a parking place not too far and went into dinner. The Dinner House wasn't crowded yet, but was filling up slowly and steadily. They were seated about the middle of the room and a little to the left. Tory could see through the doorway into the dance hall but could only see part of the room. The part she could see was the end of the bar and the bandstand. The dance floor was shiny but she could see that it had been used many times.

As they waited for the waitress, Chachi told her that she looked beautiful, that he loved her shoes. In fact, he said, she looked "Quite Sophisticated" with her hair up. She smiled and said "Thank you. You clean up rather nice, yourself. Much different with your hair combed and a clean face," she laughed. I think you are the Handsomest man in the room," She finished seriously.

"That's because most of them are much older," he said, "but I Thank You anyway. Do you want a drink, wine, beer?"

"I'll have a glass of wine," she answered. They both had a glass of red wine and before they had finished their dinner arrived. That was alright with them as they both were hungry. They smiled across the table at each other as they DINED, not much talking but many intimate smiles. The thought passed quickly through His mind, That If he were married to Tory—he's see her always across from him, everyday. Would he get tired of that? Would she always make his heart race and pound, and would his arm always ache to hold her close against his heart? Something in his face made Tory ask, quickly, "Are you okay, Chachi? Your face clouded up for a moment, is there something wrong?"

He reached across the table and took her hands in his, "Oh, no nothing wrong—you are the right one, Tory. You must know that I love you! You are the kind of woman I hoped to find. You are at ease in my house—painting, you're not afraid of ghosts, you can milk a cow, make the butter and you make me ache all over with a need I've never had before, Tory. What else can I say—I love you so very much!

She was looking at him her eyes shiny with tears. "Oh, Chachi, I would have died of a broken heart if I thought you didn't love me! I've loved you with my whole being since I saw you ride up from the river to my front porch. My heart hasn't been the same since. I ache for you, too, my Chachi." they looked at each other and both said at the same time "Let's skip the dance and go for a moonlight drive." And that is just what they did! They drove out about five miles where they stopped and danced barefoot in the moonlight to the cars stereo. He had been with girls when he was away at college, had danced, had kissed, had sex with a few, but he had *never* felt this HOT-Burning, he felt for Tory. He knew he could have her, ALL of her, tonight if he wanted to, but he wanted Tory forever, not just for a night. He wanted Tory in his house, in his bed, beside him in times of trouble, he wanted her to be the mother of his children, he wanted Tory to be his—Forever. All this he said to her there in the moonlight and she answered him with a long, hot intimate kiss and answered "Yes, Yes, My Chachi!"

They were married by a justice-of-the-peace early in the morning. They drove home and stopped at Tory's home first and woke her parents by knocking on the door and told them the news. They weren't too surprised and they congratulated them and hugged them both welcoming him to their family.

His Papa was having his breakfast with Mama there, too, when they arrived. When is Papa opened the door with a surprised but pleased look on his face. Chachi said "Papa this is Tory, the girl who lives next door to me. The one you told me to ask the Great Spirit to help me with, Well, she'll be living in MY house. We got married early this morning."

Papa's eyes misted and he hugged Chachi and then he hugged Tory. Welcome to our family and our family is small, so we expect it to get bigger now that The Great Spirit has found him a wife. "Mama," he said turning to his wife, "Look! Chachi has brought us a gift, another child to add to our family." Mama came and took Tory's hand and said, "I always wanted a little girl—I'm glad you came with Chachi. He always brought boys home before and they don't like to sew and play dolls." Tory said to her, "Tes we can sew dresses for the dolls and have tea parties." Chachi smiled at Tory and he understood that Tory now knew why he called his mother "His Child Mother."

They lived many years at the old Angelo Place. He had bought the old Slim's place when Tory's parents moved into a small town. He made more pastureland from part of it.

Chachi and his father had the biggest cattle ranch in that part of the country. Cattlemen came from many different states to buy their yearlings and bulls. They came in big trucks, loaded and hauled their cattle away to their own ranches.

Chachi and Tory had six children: three boys and three girls. They built a new two-storied house, long and wide. It was built where Tory's house was, the Old Slim place.

All their children went to college. One daughter became a Professor of Literature. The other two worked for their Business husbands.

One son became a lawyer, one became an F.B.I detective AND one became a rancher like his father and grandfather. He lived on the Old Angelo Place and helped his father raise cattle. When he was of age, he was given his own herd by his father, as his father had been, by his grandpa.

Chachi lived a long and happy life. He attributed it to Tory's love for him. He and Tory loved their children and were proud of them all.

When Tory died at age eighty-eight, she was buried in the family cemetery out on the back acre of the property. There she lay beneath her beloved oak and cedar and the rose she had planted there for Chachi's Child-Mama when she went to rest there. Papa followed soon after and lay beside her. Chachi would lay there when his time came—beside his beloved Tory. This happened when he was ninety-six.

Epilogue

His legacy lingered on for many generations. His and Papa's cattle now roamed over and on many acres of pastureland in many states. There were still horses whose shoes had the Rocking Star brand. All Papa's, Chachi's and his son, wore this brand, too.

In the land of the GREAT SPIRIT, Chachi's spirit rides his horse over his land, with his Tory riding behind him. He looks down on the land of his ancestors. He smiles at the memory of the blessings he's received and gives thanks for ALL of them, to the Great Spirit and he shouts as he rides past, "CHACHI LIVED HERE.

The End

by

Dimmon

THE WORLD OF "IN-BETWEENS"

A FEW WORDS ABOUT THE STORY—BY DIMMON

DEIDRA LIVED IN A LARGE HOUSE ON A HILL. THERE WAS A BASEMENT APARTMENT WHERE HER FATHER LIVED FOR THE FINAL FOUR YEARS OF HIS LIFE.

DEIDRA'S MOTHER WAS KILLED IN AN AUTO ACCIDENT WHICH KILLED HER AND TWO MEN IN THE OTHER CAR.

DEIDRA AND HER FRIEND HELENE WERE IN THE CAR ALSO WITH DEIDRA'S MOTHER. THE TWO OF THEM WERE IN THE HOSPITAL FOR SEVERAL WEEKS. THIS HOUSE THAT SHE LIVED IN HAD BEEN HER GRANDMOTHERS.

DEIDRA'S FATHER HAD BEFRIENDED TWO HOMELESS, BUT EDUCATED MEN, WHO STAYED OVERNIGHT, SOMETIME PLAYING DOMINOES AND CARDS. HER DAD AND THEY . . . HAD GREAT CONVERSATIONS ABOUT MANY THINGS.

DEIDRA WAS CONTENT ALONE IN THE HOUSE—until strange things BEGAN TO HAPPEN! NOISES AND ITEMS MISSING! PEOPLE IN THE APARTMENT WHO DIDN'T BELONG THERE.

HER LAST VISIT TO THE CEMETERY TO VISIT HER GRANDMOTHERS RESTING PLACE . . . . TOLD A STORY!!

The World of the "In-Betweens"

DEIDRA OWNED HER OWN ADVERTISING AGENCY—had for almost eight years. Today, was the second anniversary of her father's death and she was remembering how she wished that she had known him sooner. She was left with her grandmother when her mother was killed in an auto accident when she was eleven. He wrote her notes from all over and sent her presents of all kinds, from many places where he had been. She saw him for the first time since her mom died, when she was sixteen, on her birthday actually. The next time she saw him was when she was twenty-two, she was home for Christmas Break from college and then he was gone again—until he showed-up on her doorstep when she was thirty-five and stayed until his death two years ago. They became great Pals! He was always happy and joked a lot. IT was plain to see—that he loved her very much!

HE had explained that he was lost when her mother died. They had been married for sixteen years at that time. SO he had left her with her grandmother and he went to Europe, saw many countries, had many different jobs. He had worked as a fisherman, a baggage handler for an Airline, a guide in ATHENS, a valet to a wealthy Italian, picked grapes in Spain and helped make wine for a winery. He had been a musician since he was a young man . . . he played a saxophone in a club in France. He was there when he decided to come home to his grownup, daughter, Deidra. SHE had been DELIGHTED to see him. Today he had been gone for two years . . . tho . . . once-in-awhile, she sensed a presence in the house—not anything definite but an evasive, far-off sense of—something . . . someone. Mostly in her basement apartment where her father had lived. Once or twice as she entered the door after a shopping trip or a movie she could swear that she heard a soft note from a saxophone? When this happened, she would open the door, go down the carpeted stairs stop and listen from about half-way down look all around, but stand very still and listen. She heard nothing! She would then go back up the stairs and lock the door from her side.

The basement was already an apartment when she found this house eight years ago. It was a complete, small apartment! It even had a small fireplace in the living room. There was a door to the outside on the fireplace wall, between the fireplace and the left corner. IT WAS ALWAYS LOCKED! IT was a strong, stout, door.

The basement was divided into three separate areas, all open to each other. The kitchen was behind the living room IT Held a small refrigerator, sink, a counter with an open cupboard above it. A small drop-leaf table and two chairs. Back in the right hand corner, was a bathroom and small closet.

Today she was going to the cemetery to visit her father's grave and put flowers—But first she would have a small bite to eat. SHE had made coffee and as she was pouring a cup, she had that strange sensation, an un-easy feeling, she turned and went to the basement door. She slowly pushed it open, looked around and slowly descended the steps that whiff of—of—something rather musky reach her nose. She walked into the living room. There was her dad's sax leaning against the umbrella stand and his hat hanging on the umbrella tree. NOT A LIVING SOUL, HER!! BUT . . . the sense of a presence remained. Had the fireplace been on? It felt a bit warm down here. She walked over and checked to see if the outside door was locked. Yes, it was and the key lay there on the mantel. SHE looked into the bathroom which seemed to hold a feeling of dampness. OH! COME ON, DEIDRA—people who die, don't come back! SHE went back up, locked the door and drank her coffee and ate her Danish.

TODAY was Saturday and she was on lunch duty at the center. She served bowls of soup and MANY sandwiches and juices. Children smiled and said THANK YOU—most of the adults, too. One man in particular caught her eye. He had a beanie on his head and a VERY FAMILIAR sweater. Didn't her father have one exactly like it? with the same torn pocket? Did she give it away when he died? She had gotten rid of some of his things, but a few remained in his closet. When she had finished with this task, and went home, she would check for the sweater.

When she was finished with serving the lunches, she decided to see a matinee. A comedy which she enjoyed. Then she browsed thru a BOOKSTORE. She bought a couple to take to read in the evening. As she unlocked her door . . . she thought she heard a door being closed. She went CAUTIOUSLY thru her house looking behind doors and in closets. NOTHING but still that sense of? SHE sat down to read one of the books she had purchased, at this point remembered the sweater with the torn pocket. SHE placed her book on her chair and went to look in the basement closet—and there it was—torn pocket and all, on the umbrella tree. She hugged the sweater, sniffed it smiled to herself and went back to her book.

She was very busy this whole week. Several meetings, some sales, luncheons, etc. The owner of another advertising company, JARED SWAN, asked her out to dinner and a local Stage Play, for FRIDAY night. She, of course, said YES as he had once mentioned them working together on an advertising Campaign, so maybe that was his ulterior motive. He was there right on time to pick her up. Their dinner reservation was for six-thirty. The play began at eight-thirty. This gave them plenty of time for their dinner. The Restaurant was called "SANTOS" DOWN NEAR THE harbor. The dinner was wonderful and the man she was with was handsome and attentive. Sure enough after dinner while they were having an after dinner drink, discussing their BUSINESS, he asked if she was ready to hear his idea on their combining their advertising campaign for the Corporation he had mentioned before? He explained his ideas then asked her what she thought? She then explained her ideas to him and they had reached an agreement! NOW on to the stage play! They enjoyed the play. When they reached her house, she invited him in for a night cap. SHE had just handed him his drink when he asked "Do you have a houseguest?"

"No, why do you ask?"

"I JUST HEARD A BATHROOM FLUSH . . . DIDN'T YOU HEAR IT?"

"No, I didn't . . . I was busy with the drinks . . . and I DON'T HAVE A HOUSEGUEST!"

"MAYBE there's a television on in the house somewhere?" he asked.

"NO, AS YOU CAN SEE MY T.V. ISN'T ON, IT'S RIGHT THERE!!"

"I WOULD HAVE SWORN THAT THE TOILET FLUSHED! Well, I've got to be going, it's past my bedtime," he laughed.

"Thanks for the company for dinner and we will be getting together on the starting time for the Ads, GOODNIGHT NOW." As DEIDRA turned back into the room she listened intently for a few seconds . . . no, no one was there. With this thought she went into the basement apartment and just as the door opened, she had the strange sensation that SOMEONE HAD gone out the OUTSIDE door! She walked over to inspect. There was the key laying on the mantel in plain sight. Then she went to see the bathroom. The door was open and a towel was hanging over the towel bar. She was trying to remember the last time anyone had slept here. The best she could and the only one she could think of, was her father's friend, ROBERT AMES . . . BUT . . . when was that? LAST WINTER? He had shown up at her door and asked if he might stay the night in her Dad's room, saying that he could use a shower. Robert was one of the homeless people that her father had met when he had volunteered to help serve dinner at the Rescue Mission. HE had learned that Robert was an EDUCATED MAN WHO HAD WORKED FOR A BIG COMPANY, but just before his retirement time he was laid off along with several others. He then lost his house and his wife chose this time to leave him and move to New Jersey. He had drifted since then doing odd jobs here and there. Her father found him an interested listener who hadn't given up on life but kept on trying! HE kept up on current events of happenings around the world and he and her father were always happily discussing them. Robert would stay a day or two at a time with her father in which they played dominoes and cards. Had this towel been here since then? Surely NOT? She once more checked the outside door, climbed the stairs, and turned out the light. "Could her father's Spirit still be in his apartment? Did such things really Exist? She had read and heard that some people do believe THIS!—BUT DID SHE? She had a hard time convincing herself, she just wasn't sure! BUT, SHE WAS OPEN to turning the thought over in her head—and SUPPOSING. Her world progressed as usual. SHE and JARED SWAM DID DO A COMBINED AD PROJECT WHICH HAD WORKED OUT WELL FOR BOTH OF THEM.

DEIDRA had a best friend, FRANCINE, who had been her friend since they both were eleven. They were very close in age. They were born in the same year . . . DEIDRA on DECEMBER 13th AND FRANCINE ON DECEMBER 15th. In fact—both had been in the accident that killed DEIDRA's mother. BOTH WERE IN THE HOSPITAL FOR MONTHS before they were released. IT was at this time that Deidra was released to her grandmother, and her father chose to leave. The girls were constantly together after this. They went to the same drama School. They needed to keep busy to keep their minds off the accident. They enjoyed doing the plays—but as time went by, they enjoyed watching rather than performing. Francine became a Drama Coach and loved it!

This Friday DEIDRA was going to see a play in the City where Francine's school was located. They planned to spent the weekend just relaxing and enjoying their time together. They decided to watch a movie, an old one that they loved. They were both engrossed in it when suddenly they heard the toilet flush. They started for the basement with a fireplace poker in each of their hands. Deidra opened the door, hit the light switch and they both scanned the room. No one was in sight and the bathroom door stood open . . . wide! They carefully and slowly went on down into the room. Not a thing did they see, BUT . . . the sweater with the torn pocket was gone from the peg it always hung on. Deidra made straight for the outside door only to find it securely locked! "I don't understand this, who could be in here and HOW did they get in?" ASKED DEIDRA.

"DO you smell a musky smell—like a man's cologne? Did your Dad use a musk cologne?"

"NO, Never that I smelled but I did smell it here a few weeks ago.

IT's a strange situation here at your house, Deidra, maybe you should check into WHO owned this house before you bought it. Actually, who owned it BEFORE the person YOU BOUGHT IT FROM!! Maybe there's a secret entrance. Maybe there IS a person beside yourself!

Don't even suggest such a thing!, FRANCINE, I'll be too frightened to even unlock the basement! BUT I will see if I can find out WHO owned it before I bought it from MR. BOYD. I just automatically though tit was his family home, that he had inherited it. Come on, let's go to bed. I have an extra bed in my room, Francine, you're welcome to sleep there, if you want to.

"YES, I think I'll take you up on the offer!"

THEY SLEPT WELL, never heard another note from the sax nor did they hear the toilet flush. FRANCINE DID wake up before DEIDRA and she *did* wander out into the kitchen and made herself a cup of coffee before Deidra arose.

Today they were going horseback riding out in the countryside. They rented two horses for the morning. THEY RODE DOWN TO the creek and put their feet in the water while they ate their sandwiches they had brought with them. They rode up a mountain trail for a half mile or so, to watch squirrels search for seeds and nuts in the trees and birds being chased from the tree by them. THE mountainside was covered in beautiful colors and wildflowers. IT WAS a lovely spring day! THEY sat on a log discussing where they were in life.

"ARE we ever going to find the LOVE OF OUR LIFE," asked Francine. "Look how long we've been alone—don't you think we should be looking for a mate to spend our OLD AGE TIME WITH? We're forty-two, or will be on our birthday. REMEMBER TERRANCE, THE man I almost married a few years ago? I really should have married him and not have kept thinking that maybe there was another someone for me. I gave him up—and now he's happily married to a lovely girl and they have two children to leave to the world isn't that sad, Deidra?" S HE saw that FRANCINE was crying. "WELL, I've not yet met anyone to HAVE left behind—so you are ahead of me, FRANCINE, BUT we're not too old to find someone, yet, so don't cry—just keep looking for him—keep your eyes open! He'll come along!"

Deidra dropped Francine off and she stopped at the mall to sit and watch people, one of her favorite things to do. People walking hand in hand and some with children. She would like a man—to sit and converse with, play games, make love and to have coffee with each morning, someone to cuddle up to on cold nights. BUT she didn't feel too bad about being by herself—OR about having no children. YES, she could at least be aware, JUST IN CASE he should appear and she be unaware of him being the one!

THERE WERE TIMES when she heard the low sax music from the stereo. She'd go down and turn it off. Maybe there was a short in the wiring sometimes as she turned to go she'd notice that the old sweater was gone from its peg. She kept wondering how the hell did it keep disappearing and appearing?

ONE MORNING AS SHE WALKED TO HER CAR, she spied the man she had seen at the RESCUE MISSION WHEN SHE HAD SERVED LUNCH THERE. The same she and Francine had seen at the diner, the one who had smiled at her and wore a sweater EXACTLY like her dad's, torn pocket and all. He was OR looked as if he had just come out thru the door, although IT was closed tightly.

He held up the Newspaper and asked "Is it okay if I take the Newspaper with me? I want to read an article and this is yesterdays Newspaper?"

"Yes, take it and enjoy, was her answer."

HIS NEXT WORDS SURPRISED HER "DO YOU THINK IT WOULD BE OKAY IF I went into the apartment of your dad's AND MAKE A CUP OF COFFEE? I WON'T MESS anything up . . . I'll be neat. I MISS YOUR FATHER. WE HAD GREAT TIMES TOGETHER . . . I DON'T THINK HE WOULD MIND MY HAVING A CUP OF COFFEE."

Deidre looked at him in disbelief "What a strange request! Was he serious? HE looked directly into her eyes and somehow she knew THAT IF her dad was there, he'd say, "Why not let him have his coffee, Deidre?" SO she told him to wait and she would unlock the door for him, which she did and he thanked her and said "I'LL BE NEAT." "When you go just close the door behind you, it locks when it closes. Make sure you close it when you leave. I'll be back soon. Enjoy your coffee and I left a coffee cake on the table for you to have with your coffee. IT'S FROM DAD," she said. SHE had an appointment with a new company about doing a layout for them. She got the contract and was out of there in about ninety minutes. She had the contract and would have the money MONDAY—SHE was feeling very happy! SHE decided to go by the cemetery and visit her DAD and later, her grandmother. They were in the same cemetery and so was her mother AND the two little girls who were in the car with her. SHE didn't know where they were in the cemetery. She stopped at her Dad's first. "HELLO DAD, ONE OF YOUR FRIENDS STOPPED BY YOUR PLACE FOR A CUP OF COFFEE. I LEFT HIM THERE WHILE I VISIT. I EXPLAINED TO HIM THAT THE DOOR LOCKED AUTOMATICALLY IF HE LEFT BEFORE I RETURNED. HE SAYS HE MISSES YOU. AS IT OKAY THAT I LET HIM IN FOR HIS COFFEE, DAD? I

HOPE SO. I WILL SAY I LOVE YOU AND GO SAY HELLO TO
GRANDMOTHER. I'VE NOT BEEN THERE FOR AWHILE.
BYE FOR NOW."

She parked her car at the end of row B. Look at all the graves of
children! Even babies lay here she thought as she came to number
#13 which was grandmother's. "HELLO GRANDMOTHER. GEE!
I NEVER NOTICED HOW MANY CHILDREN AND BABIES
ARE NEAR YOU. I IMAGINE YOU ARE HAPPY HERE. YOU
WERE A GREAT GRANDMOTHER, I DON'T KNOW HOW
I WOULD HAVE MADE WITHOUT YOU. I LOVE YOU
GRANDMOTHER. I MUST GO NOW THO, AS THERE'S A
GUEST AT MY HOUSE. SAYING THIS, SHE TURNED AND
WALKED TO HER CAR AND DROVE ON HOME.

She parked her car and went inside, put her contract and
money safely away and went to make herself a cup of tea. She
heard sax music then remembered that her dad's friend was below.
She unlocked the basement door, looked around. She saw no
one *but* the music played soft and low. She slowly advanced to
the bottom of the stairs and into the room. It was empty, BUT
as promised, very neat and clean. She could faintly smell the
musky evasive odor. On the table she found a note which said: "I
THANK YOU SO MUCH FOR THE COFFEE CAKE AND
COFFEE. I'VE ALWAYS LOVED IT HERE. SOMEHOW I
FIND IT COMFORTING—LIKE WHEN YOUR DAD LIVED
HERE. I SEEM TO SENSE HIS PRESENCE IN THIS ROOM,
ALTHOUGH I KNOW HE'S BEEN GONE FOR TWO YEARS.
THIS WAS THE ONLY HOME I EVER HAD IT WAS SUCH
A BLESSING THAT I MET YOUR DAD . . . I COUNT HIM
AS MY BEST FRIEND. HE ALWAYS SAID THAT HE HAD A
WONDERFUL DAUGHTER. AND I MUST AGREE. THANK
YOU, AGAIN," SIGNED ROBERT ADAMS. She walked over,
hugged the torn-pocket sweater, touched the sax and turned the
music off.

As she got upstairs she remembered and *Hoped* that Francine was not despairing over having never been married and that she had no children! She wanted her friend, Francine, to be happy and contented—like she was.

She took out the cards from the drawer and played a game or two of solitaire before her cup of tea—then she lay down upon her bed and dreamed of grandmother rocking "a lap full of" babies. IN THE OLD ROCKING CHAIR that still sat in her bedroom.

She and Francine would be having their birthdays before long.

THANKSGIVING was coming soon. She thought she might have a few people in for a THANKSGIVING DINNER at her place. She would invite Francine, James, one of the single men from her company, Emiline from the BEAUTY SHOP and Thomas MC EBBE from the Academy OF Drama . . . a friend of Francine's. She Might even invite her father's friend Robert Adams . . . he would enjoy it so much!

On Friday she handed out invitations to James, Emiline and Thomas McEBBE. She left the invitation at the Rescue Mission to be given to Robert when he came for dinner later in the evening. ON TUESDAY she got confirmation from all—except Robert Adams. There was still a week left so hopefully he would call!

She kept busy planning her dinner menu. She had plenty of room for the number of people she had invited to DINE at her dining room table. SHE would use her WHITE CHINA AND HER BLUE CRYSTAL. She would use her REAL SILVER THAT had been her Grandmother's. She had polished it to a high shine, cups were white with gold trim for the dessert coffee.

Finally, a few days before Thanksgiving, Mister ROBERT ADAMS called at her door saying that he would be delighted to come—but he had no proper clothing to wear and he wouldn't want to embarrass her or himself, or her guest.

"I understand," said Deidra, "but you have been a friend of dad's, and he really enjoyed your company, he wouldn't mind if you wore something of his. HE WAS ABOUT YOUR SIZE, Robert, so if you want to, why don't you go down and see if there is anything you could or would—wear. I'm sure he would not mind at all, in face, he'd be glad to loan something to you—go on down now and look thru his closet and choose something you like and take it with you now, or better yet—why don't you come the night before THANKSGIVING AND SPENT THE NIGHT IN DAD'S PLACE AND YOU CAN DRESS THERE FOR DINNER. How would that be Robert? Dad would have agreed to that, I believe."

"WELL if you think that will be okay—I'd like that very much!

"OK, I'll see you on THANKSGIVING," said DEIDRA. He reached out his hand to her and thanked her so much for inviting him. "It's a long time since I'VE SPENT A Thanksgiving with a group of friends in the home of a friend." He walked off whistling softly.

She went to bed exhausted from her planning. In fact, she took a Tylenol because she had gotten a headache.

She awoke sometime after one P.M. to sax music from below. She listened for any other sound but heard none. She put on her robe and slippers and quietly opened the basement door and stood there in shock! For now below, in the living room was her Dad playing his sax! She let out a scream and when she did the sax player turned her way and she saw that it was Robert Adams in her father's robe and PJ. HOW did he get in and WHY? She half closed the basement door by pulling without realizing why she was closing it. She immediately reopened it—to an empty apartment. Where had he gone? She called his name, Robert where are you? She got no answer.

"I'M coming down to speak with you. How did you get in?" SHE SEARCHED ALL OVER THE APARTMENT AND FOUND NO ONE, BUT when she checked behind the bathroom door, on the hook where her dad hung his robe and pajamas—they both were missing! WHERE HAD ROBERT DISAPPEARED TO? WAS HE REALLY A GHOST?

NO, she knew Robert Adams was real. She had seen him with her DAD and just yesterday she had talked to him herself. WHAT in the world was happening? SHE checked the door—it was locked. How could these things be happening?—OR—was her mind playing tricks on her? She went slowly up the stairs looking over her shoulder to make sure if she had REALLY seen anyone. She locked the door from HER side tonight!

Two days later she went to pick up her newspaper where it had landed near the lilac bush beside the outside door of the basement, and found her father's house slippers placed slightly underneath the backside of the lilac bush. NOW, HOW HAD THEY GOTTEN OUTSIDE AND WHO HAD PUT THEM THERE? What was going on right here in her own house? HER basement? In her dad's part of the house. Did someone live there still? She had seen her father laid to rest, so it couldn't BE HIM or could it?

She filled most of her day today planning menus, washing her crystal and the set of china she was to use for her dinner. Today was the day she did her special orders for the pies or there would be none left.

This was the day for cleaning the downstairs apartment. She took the vacuum out of the closet and vacuumed the living room. Next she mopped the kitchen and bath. The kitchen was clean. No dirty dishes, clean microwave, and two towels and a washcloth in the hamper. She dusted everywhere, picked up the towels and washcloth and put them in the washroom upstairs. She put fresh towels out and then put the vacuum in the closet and went back upstairs.

I wonder who did own this house? WHO BUILT IT? She decided to make a call to MR. BOYD and ask about the house. The phone rang three times before it was answered.

"HELLO, MR. BOYD here, How may I HELP YOU?"

"MR. BOYD, it's DEIDRA WILLIAMS WHO BOUGHT A HOUSE FROM YOU eight years ago—the one with the apartment that fills the whole basement—it's on ROSE HILL."

"OH! YES, I REMEMBER you. HOW MAY I HELP YOU?"

"I WAS WONDERING WHO OWNED THE HOUSE BEFORE YOU, AND WAS THE BASEMENT ROOM THERE THEN?"

"YES, I BELIEVE IT WAS—most of it anyway. I think the bathroom and fireplace were built about the same time. Why do you ask, is it falling apart or?"

"Oh! no nothing like that but who first owned it, do you know?"

"LETS SEE. I BELIEVE IT WAS FIRST BOUGHT ABOUT THIRTY-EIGHT YEARS AGO BY A MR. AND MRS. ELIGAH STONE. They owned it for many years." DEIDRA WAS STUNNED! ELIGAH STONE WAS HER GRANDFATHER! BUT SHE HAD LIVED WITH HER GRANDMOTHER AFTER HER MOTHER DIED. HAD IT BEEN IN THIS HOUSE? BUT I THOUGHT I BOUGHT IT EIGHT YEARS AGO. What was happening to her life, her memory, her safe footing? She didn't remember this as her grandmother's house. She didn't even remember her grandfather? WHY?

"ARE YOU OKAY MISS WEBB," asked MR. BOYD. IS THERE ANYTHING I CAN DO?"

"No, thanks OH! did you know that there is a stereo system built into the fireplace mantel?"

"Actually, I didn't there was no mantel at first, just a small fireplace. The family had the mantel put on later, WHY?

"Well, things seem to happen down there—sometimes. Were there any strange sounds or happenings that you know of back then?"

"It's an old house, Deidra, and old houses have strange noises. But to answer your question, nothing was said to me about strange noises Or music playing. Didn't your DAD live there when he died? Maybe he doesn't want to leave—yet. I'VE heard of such things.

But I've never known anyone myself personally. But—who knows? Keep me posted, ok? Bye now."

A lot of good that call did thought Deidra. Maybe I'll go one of these days and look to see when it was built and by whom.

It was the weekend before THANKSGIVING and Deidra had her turkey and dressing to be made. Her yams, pumpkin pie and her pecan pie were already baked. She had her gravy mixes in an upper cabinet, ready to be made. She was READY for THANKSGIVING.

On Tuesday afternoon Robert Adams called with a strange request "Would it be okay to bring Ronald Jones with him to sleep over in her DAD's apartment? You remember Ronald? He and I stayed here a few times with Walter and played games, so is it ok if Ronald stays, too? He has no family except me and your dad—we were all—family."

DEIDRA smiled to herself and thought—Why not? "Sure," she answered, and if he needs to borrow some of Dad's clothes for the day—he may do so. So he will be here for dinner then—right?"

"Yes, if it's alright?"

Her dinner went fine! Robert and RONALD looked very neat! They joined in the conversation of the Advertising Business discussions which surprised everyone by their knowledge on the subject. NONE OF them, including Deidra, knew that Ronald's degree was in Business. Thomas had worked for almost twenty years, where he was head of a department of Managing, SO THEY enjoyed being in on the conversation. They had just begun their dessert when from the basement came the saxophone music. "Shall I GO TURN IT OFF FOR YOU," asked ROBERT.

"Yes, please do," answered Deidra and he left to turn the music off. Deidra explained to the rest of her guests, that the stereo system had a short of some kind and played at the most inappropriate times—a little unnerving—late at night!

After dinner they all agreed to play a table game with dice that the whole group could sit together and play at the game table in Deidra's den. They played until almost 11:30. They had stopped for a coffee break around Ten P.M. then they finished the rest of the game—their final game for the evening. Everyone said they had enjoyed the dinner And the company of all. Deidra walked them to the door, said goodnight and Thanked them for coming—all except Thomas and RONALD who were going to stay one more night in her Dad's apartment in the basement. She told them they could have breakfast before they left the next morning. She had left food in the refrigerator and coffee was there ready to plug in.

As Deidra straightened her kitchen, she kept seeing the face of Robert Adams—shaved clean, his haircut and dressed in her DAD's clothes she could see that he had a nice firm body and his knowledge of Business and advertising was all a surprise to her. IT WAS too bad they had fallen thru the cracks—he should be working at some nice place where he could be proud of himself. How could she help him? Could she offer him a job? In her business? Could he handle it? AND would he want to work for a woman? She decided to ask him! As she got to the bottom of the stairs she heard the sound of a razor and thru the open bathroom door, Thomas was standing there in his boxer shorts. She was turning to go back up the stairs, when he turned the razor off and turned to face her. "I'M SO SORRY TO HAVE barged in on you, Robert, it was rude of me." He put the razor away and walked out of the bathroom "I was going to put on my pajamas, it's okay—both of us are old enough to have seen people in their underwear, so no harm done," he said as he pulled his pajamas up. "What do you want?" Deidra was so aware of him being a male and she had admired his body, standing there in his underwear and his hair wet and full of curl from his shower. She must have looked befuddled for he asked "Are you ok? What do you want?"

She couldn't believe her thoughts! What I WANT IS FOR YOU TO HOLD ME IN YOUR ARMS AND LET ME GRAB A HANDFUL OF YOUR WET, CURLY HAIR. For a moment she thought she had said it out loud from the expression on his face. "Come," he said, "let's sit and have a last cup of hot tea—you look a little pale. Maybe you worked too hard on the THANKSGIVING DINNER?"

"Well, I am a little tired—but I want to talk to you for a few minutes, about giving you a job in my Advertising Company."

He had stopped, holding the two cups and was staring in disbelief at her. "WHY, AFTER ALL THIS TIME I've known your DAD and spent time here with him, ARE YOU ASKING ME NOW!

She was staring at him and answered "I never knew how Much you know about my business until today—at the Dinner how *Really* educated you are—and how Really handsome you are! SO, do you want a job with my company, ROBERT? A woman needs a man who can help her run her business and maybe teach her a few new tricks of the trade. How about it Robert?"

"DOES this apartment go with the job? and maybe your friends who MIGHT need a good Business Man—I'm sure Ronald could handle that, for some smaller business. HE CLEANS UP NICE, TOO, HE SAIS On SUNDAY, with a feeling of being out of step and a strangeness, Deidra went out to the cemetery to visit her father's gravesite. She placed flowers there, sat for a few minutes—BUT grandmother seemed to be calling her. She said goodbye to her father and went to the place, among the babies and children, where grandmother lay resting. The uneasiness was stronger as she neared. Once again she noticed the babies buried near and around grandmother. I Wonder Why She Was laid here amongst the children, thought Deidra? She began to walk along reading the headstones; A baby girl ten months old, A two year old little boy named Alex, Thirteen month old twins—DANIEL and SAMUEL. Deidra wondered what was the reason for their death?

WHAT DO CHILDREN DO WHEN THEY DIE? DO THEY LIVE IN HEAVEN? DO ANY OF THEM *WISH* TO BE BACK ON EARTH? AND *WHAT* WOULD THEY DO *IF* THEY

DID COME BACK? DO THEY GROW UP IN HEAVEN AND COME BACK AS AN ADULT?

She had walked farther and farther away from her grandmother's resting place—When Suddenly she froze in her tracks!

THE HEADSTONE WAS OF WHITE MARBLE WITH A WOOLY LAMB AND DOVES. TWO CHILDREN WERE BURIED HERE. THEN HER HEART STOPPED FOR A SECOND, SHE COULD HARDLY BREATHE!—THE INSCRIPTION READ: "HERE LIES OUR DEIDRA AND HER BEST FRIEND HELENE, WHO ARE NOW ANGELS IN HEAVEN, BURIED HERE BESIDE A MOTHER TO WATCH OVER THEM, and next to this grave was Deidra's Mom's gravesite, AND next to her were two men: Robert Adams and Ronald Ebbe who had died in the same accident.

She stood stricken in disbelief and silence! THIS CAN'T be, she thought. Helene And I DIDN'T DIE! We *were* IN THE HOSPITAL for weeks. My dad lived with me for four years before he died—I own my own business and a home. How Can This Be True?

She turned, running to her car, drove home, parked and went inside—and there were her friends—Robert, Ronald and Helene. It was then that Deidra joined the world of the ones caught in a realm called The World of THE IN-BETWEEN!

THE END

THE LYON'S DEN

AQ

A HIKING TRIP UP TO AN OLD ABANDONED CABIN LEADS VICTORIA AND JAMES INTO INTRIGUE OF UNTOLD DANGER AND SUSPENSE. A SECRET MILITARY INSTALLATION_____-DESERTED??? WHY???

BY DIMMON

The Lyon's Den

Victoria was a tall, beautiful, thin girl—well she was a little more than a girl. She was now a twenty-two year old woman—who had her own business, A Shoe Business . . . women and men. Nice expensive ones.

Victoria's mother had left her father when Victoria was a little girl of three years. Her father was a military man, who was gone most of the time, to al parts of the world. He was killed last year in an accident. Just as he was getting ready to retire after twenty-five years of military. The only thing good, if you could call it good, was the insurance he had left her.

She worked, Physically in her Shop besides taking care of the business end of it, too. She had majored in Business in College, so she was quite capable of handling this. She had owned her place for two years, now, and it was improving in its sales. She was happy with her life.

She belonged to a group of women who worked out on Monday nights. She had Jazz Dancing each Wednesday and Friday nights. She went there with a group of friends that she had grown-up with—both men and women. A few of them were couples. There was one single male named, James, who was usually, her escort, since she was one of the two single women of the group, and Estelle usually "found" her own escort, never or hardly ever the same one. She was a stage actress and a dance teacher. She was the most outgoing one of the group, a little too much once in a while, especially if she had more than three drinks—she was Not a drinker!

One weekend James asked her if she would like to go out of town for the weekend—up to his cabin in the mountains? Victoria loved the cabin, in fact she loved the out of doors. She had spent lots of time on hiking trails when she was a teenager, so the idea sounded great to her. So Friday evening found them in James Jeep Cherokee on their way to his cabin.

I guess this is a good time to explain about James. His house was on the block behind Victoria's. Their backyards were a fence apart. His back fence was also her backyard fence. The house had stood vacant for almost a year. An older couple lived there when Victoria and her Dad first moved into *their* house. The old couple loved Victoria and had her over for dinner, table games and occasionally, a game of croquet in their backyard. Victoria was only nine at this time and had a nanny who took care of her when her dad was away on business. The old couple moved, when Victoria was thirteen, to a Senior Complex. She missed them terribly! The house was again vacant for eight or mine months and—James' family moved in! From then on, Victoria's life changed. She was no longer lonely! All she had to do was go into her backyard and there was James—read to keep her company. They became the Best of Friends and still were and would always be. She learned to climb a tree, how to fly a kite, to skate and how to swim really well. He had given her her first kiss, loved it when her breast developed and asked to see them. She said "NO, way! James! girls don't show their breasts!" He promised that he wouldn't touch them—just look. So, one day up in the tree house—she showed him. He was in Awe and thanked her for showing him. He always admired them but never asked to see them again. They were friends and had been since way back then, and now were in his jeep going to his cabin.

James father had bought the cabin years ago and had updated it some. He had added a front porch to sit and watch the sunsets. He also added a loft bedroom. There was a bedroom in the cabin, already, but James Daddy had added the loft for James bedroom. The cabin was at a two thousand feet elevation. Very nice in the daytime but cold at night. Covers were a necessity at night . . . and pajamas.

Victoria had brought her Levis, her boots for hiking and a sweat shirt, her Pajamas and a Mackinaw jacket. You never knew when you might need one. She and James planned a hike up to an old abandoned cabin, a large one There was a well of water, an old barn and a field of about an acre and a half that was full of all kinds of Creatures. James and Victoria had hiked up there once, a few years ago but the incline is steep and much higher elevation than James' cabin. Some thick woods to go through and no water until you get there. It was about a three hour hike. They had spent the night there the first time they had gone, and planned to do the same this time. The old woodstove was there and quite capable of holding a fire The kitchen and living room were in good shape, for having been empty. In fact, they had commented on that fact on their trip before. James had mentioned that it seemed that someone had taken care of the cabin. They hadn't even gone into the barn as a section of its roof had fallen in—a large portion of it. They had spent their time in the cabin—painting and photographing from the porch and front yard. James had said that "someone" had mentioned, in passing, that the old cabin was haunted, but James had chalked that up to LORE. They hadn't seen anything to frighten them when they were there before.

They reached James cabin, unloaded the Jeep and checked on logs for the fireplace, which were always brought in before the winter arrived. James paid a Mr. Ripley, who lived down the mountain a few miles, to make sure that there was wood for the fireplace. James called him the day before they left home and sure enough—here were the logs.

After they were settled in, had shaken the covers to make sure there were no spiders lurking there. The kitchen had its propane cook stove, and a water faucet over the sink. At this time of year, it worked wonderfully! Victoria made tea while James brought in the wood. Soon they were out on the porch drinking their tea and crackers, watching the beautiful Sunset. As night came, they put on their sweat-suits and watched as the sky filled with stars. It was a clear, beautiful night Sky. About ten, they went inside, got dressed for bed and brushed their teeth. James gave Victoria the bathroom first. She came out in her pajamas aid goodnight, kissed his cheek and went to the bedroom. Her eyes closed immediately. She never even heard James go up into the loft room.

She awoke to the smell of bacon and coffee. James had awaken first and was already in the kitchen cooking. Victoria got her robe and wandered out into the kitchen. "Hello, Sleepy Head" James said as he kissed her cheek and put is arms around her waist. "Did you sleep well?" he asked her. "Like a baby" she replied as she sat down at the table where her coffee awaited her. James set her plate in front of her and placed his across from hers. "What's on our agenda for today?" she asked?

"Well, the field of flowers, butterflies and birds await," he said, "and I brought my camera." James was a photographer for a Nature Magazine. They finished their breakfast and while James got his equipment ready, she did the dishes. They walked slowly across and thru the field. The poppies and the lavender and wildflowers of many different kinds made the most beautiful natural carpet. There were a few small scattered trees in bloom and the birds were all over them, flying to and from. A large eagle soared overhead and Victoria wondered if he knew what a magnificent sight he was! The whole place cast a magic spell this early! James was busy taking his photos. A few squirrel ran out from the trees and away thru the flowery field. Victoria found a tree stump where some tree had once stood and sat down to enjoy the view. Past the fields was the beginning of a shallow canyon. She could see a few treetops. James was busy for another hour with his camera.

At lunchtime, Victoria unpacked their picnic basket. She had brought tea in bottles, crackers and cheese and apples. James took time out to join her picnic luncheon. He told her that he loved her keeping hi company, and that he loved her dearly! She smiled and told him she felt the same way about him. He went back to his photography and Victoria took her paints from the Jeep, and did a quick painting of one of the trees with a bluebird sitting on one of the branches. She thought she might take it back and show it to the girls at their next ART gathering.

They wandered back to the cabin about two-thirty and just KICKED BACK. No TV here, but there was a wall of books in a large shelf. Maybe play a game of checkers Or dominoes. They decided on reading. They sat on separate chairs rather than the couch or loveseat. This way they could just relax while they read. James looked up and asked "Shall we hike up to the 'Haunted Cabin' tomorrow? Why not," agreed Victoria.

So they arose to seven a.m. and started their ascent up the trail to the abandoned cabin, Or the Haunted Cabin, as James called it. It was a beautiful day, not too hot and there was a light breeze. The trail was a low grade upward, but always upward.

They reached the cabin about eleven thirty. James pushed on the door and same as their trip before, it opened. It looked the same as it did before on the inside, too. But—did she smell something—strange—or, or—unusual—anything strange, she asked?

"Only a musty oil cabin smell is all I detect" replied James. Really, Victoria what can one expect when the cabin is used only once every two or so years? Doesn't the cabin look clean to have been closed for quite a while? Maybe some other hikers did Or do come by and use it for a day or two."

"Let's rest for a little while, James, before we go out to paint and photograph, Okay?"

"Sure, said James, meanwhile I'll look around for snakes or Black Widow spiders."

"Don't tease about that, James!" said Vicki. They sat and closed their eyes just relaxed for about forty minutes. Then Vicki got her paints and James got his camera and they went to see what lay behind the cabin and old falling down barn with its broken roof: Behind it they found more of Nature's gifts to photograph and to paint. Out back of the old cabin about a half-mile was a creek. There they found a beaver busily building, working very hard to make his dam. A big black crow kept diving down at him. He tried to ignore it at first, but it kept on torturing him until he dived under and into his house. The crow then decided to start a fight with a hawk. They flew up, circled each other and the crow dived for the hawk, but the hawk managed to evade the crow and turned to attack the crow. They were entangled in battle for a few minutes, feathers flew and they each made their Battle Cries, but the crow lost its grip and the hawk flew high, high, and higher and rose to heights the crow couldn't. He flew away defeated and hungry. James has gotten this whole thing on film. Victoria was watching James Film when something caught her eye—something way down in the sloping canyon and beyond. What was it? IT looked like a flash from the sun hitting a mirror, perhaps a car window? but there was no road that Far below! The Old Dirt road was much higher up. She asked James if he had seen it. "No," he hadn't seen anything. "There's really no telling what it was, Vicki, that's WAY DOWN, in the lower canyon." The grassy slope was at least thirty feet wide and then it dropped to a lower level which also sloped toward the canyon's edge. This piece of ground was also at least, twice thirty feet. Then it dropped off into the canyon. At this point of the beginning slope, one could barely see the canyon floor which was very, very deep! From there—the flash of light had come. They walked back to have the lunch they had packed, both were hungry.

"Maybe you saw the GHOST of The Cabin," joked James. All Haunted Cabins have ghosts, don't they?"

"This is no time to be talking about ghosts—you know that there is no such thing as ghosts—it's all just LORE, like your Dad said. Can we go back to your cabin now, James?"

"Well, I'd hate to leave without at least one picture of the ghost," said James trying not to laugh.

Victoria was beginning to get just a little aggravated with his teasing. She had this strange feeling of "Something" she just couldn't put her mind to rest. Of course she hadn't told James how she felt.

"I just don't feel relaxed, James. Do you still want more photos—if so—you should be out shooting, it's getting late for your Nature shots. Where Are you planning to shoot next, and What?"

"I'd like a few shots of and around the old barn, but you don't need to come if you don't want to, you can stay in the cabin and rest. I'll be back in a few minutes, said James. "I have my gun strapped one—don't worry." He took his camera and left her there in the cabin. She took her book that she had brought, sat down on the big old chair and began to read.

Soon her eyes closed as did her book.

When she awoke she saw that the shadows were lengthening and it was late, too late! and where was James?

Vicki put on her sweatshirt and walked out toward the Old Barn. There was no sight of James. She called his name but got no answer. She walked on around to the back of the barn where the roof had fallen loose and hanging down to the ground. She called his name again, and thought she heard him. At that instant she saw his camera laying just inside, on the left hear, the hanging roof. James would NEVER lay his camera down just anywhere. Where was He? Once more she called his name—louder this time. She heard him groan! She moved cautiously forward and around the hanging roof and there he lay. He had a cut on his head, blood all over and he had twisted his knee—she could see. His gun was still in his holster. Immediately she began to look around for a way to get him back to the cabin. WHEELS, she needed wheels, wagon, a cart, *didn't all farms* have some sort of wagon? She entered the barn and began to look. In the far, west corner she found it—a wagon. She had to remove some old towsacks from it. Now, she needed something to lay across the top of the wagon. She found it!—a small door. Now to get James up off the floor and onto the door! She decided to put him on the door first, and then lift and slide the door with James on it—up onto the wagon. She laid the door down and gently by lifting and sliding—he was on the door. Next, she braked the wagon's wheels, until she got James' ?? right behind the wagon. Head near the wagon's rear and she lifted it up onto the back part of the wagon. She then went to the front of the wagon, leaned over, and with both her hands, one on either side, lifted and slid the door with James, forward until the door with him on it—was balanced enough for her to pull him to the cabin.

Thank God the porch was low! She parked the wagon's front as close as possible to the porch and once more she lifted the door with James, sat it on the porch, and pushed it until it was secure on the porch. Then she pulled and pushed it with James, thru the cabin door, into the living room. Next she got the bottle of whiskey she had discovered earlier in one of the cupboards, and cleaned the head wound. It wasn't as serious as she had first imagined. She took the tealeaves from the pot made a poultice. She placed it on the Wound, using James big bandana to tie it into place. Next she went to the knee—no breaks, just a bad sprain! She poured whiskey on this would also, and bandaged it tightly with a part of the tablecloth they had brought from James' cabin. He awoke at this time and asked "What Happened?"

"That's what I'd like to know," answered Victoria, What happened to you at the Old Barn? I found you laying inside the barn where the roof touches the ground. Your camera was over against the west side of the barn, just inside. WHAT did Happen to you, James?" Victoria asked, her eyes full of tears.

James began to explain, "I was just about ready to come back to the cabin, when I spied a large beautiful coyote enter the Old Barn, so I quietly entered in the back where the roof hangs down. I was focusing my camera to make the shot, when suddenly he caught the scent of me turned, snarling and charged. I stumbled on an old rake laying there and went down, twisting my leg and as he charged, something fell from above and hit my head. That is the last that I remember. "How did you get me here from the barn?" he asked.

"Well, that's another story altogether—we'll leave it for later.—It's a good thing that you have lost a little weight this year.—I was lucky to get you here. We are now in deep trouble. You have a sprained knee and a head wound, and We have a three hour hike back to your cabin. You are in no condition to hike. What will we do for food? There is water, of course, and I've checked the pantry and cabinets in the kitchen. There are a few cans of meat, some oatmeal, beans and rice, four cans of vegetables, a box of tea and one of coffee, a small can of sugar and flour. There are a few utensils; a skillet, two bent pans, a can-opener, a hand one, of course, a pancake turner, a meat fork, and a can of Lard! We will probably be okay for a day or two—What will we do then, James? there is no road in here—except the old rut of one out back a half mile or so and IT's A DANGEROUS OLD Road! It hasn't been used for some years now. I'd be afraid to drive on it! Even IF I did—how could you make it out to the Old road? There's the wagon, of course, I could possibly pull you—Victoria stopped—out of breath.

You know what, Vicki—you are nervous—when you go on with a lengthy explanation—you are tired or scared. How about us just waiting it out here for a couple of days, see how I do, THEN you may have to go bring the jeep up the old road and "CART ME TO IT." We did come up to relax, paint and take pictures. WE'll be alright for a couple of days. What do you say, my friend, y Vicki?

"I guess I CAN paint from the porch and you can sit out there with your camera and watch for the Woodland Creatures. Maybe the coyote will return. I really would like to have a nice photograph of him. He was a handsome coyote! An Awesome sight when he is charging! Frightening, too, tho," said James. "Hey! maybe we can find me a crutch!—a forked branch! from a tree, I could do that! Can you find me one, Vicki?"

She looked at him and as mulch as she loved him—right now she'd like to push him down! He wanted Her to find a branch for him to use as a crutch! It was better, she decided suddenly, than having to tow him around in the wagon. So Victoria went hunting for a branch-crutch. It took her awhile to find just the right one, but she finally did! She peeled all the small off and smoothed it the best she could. She brought it into James. "OH, great job Vicki, I'm so glad I taught you long ago how to use a hunting knife. Nice job you did," he said. "Thank You. How about some breakfast, I'm awfully hungry."

"There's coffee and flour, baking powder here, but I've never actually made biscuits—would you settle for pancakes—I found honey in the pantry," said Vicki.

"Oh, that will be great—especially the coffee," said James. Half hour later found them eating. "Not bad," said James, "I was really hungry!" As Victoria came from the kitchen after finishing up there, she asked, "What about the coyote you found in the barn, is he a harmful element we have to contend with for the next two days?"

"I don't really think so. I think he was just protecting himself, he wasn't trying to hurt me—he was trying to get away from me and I, myself, tripped and fell. He probably lives in the barn."

Let's go out on the porch now. I'll take the chairs from the kitchen out there for us to sit on. We'll take your camera and my paints. They had been out for a couple of hours—Vicki had painted a picture of the wagon. She had used to bring James from the old barn. Squirrels and chipmunks had scampered across the yard and up and down the trees. A big turtle even crawled slowly out to the center and sunned himself. A mother rabbit with babies ran past, and then about three who should walk out on the far end of the yard, sit himself down, give a big yawn—but Mr. Coyote. James got a few shots of him. Victoria started to pain him, but he left—just as Vicki was about to paint his hindquarters—he arose, stretched and sauntered off toward the barn.

They sat out for another hour or so and as the day was ending they went inside. Vicki took the chairs back to the kitchen, and made tea. When she came back into the living room James had managed to move a small table that had been against the walk, over to sit near their big chairs. He had dominoes on the table. Victoria brought the snack cracker and cheese from their knapsack they had brought their food in, then the dominoes game began! They played one game and had started another when they decided they were too tired and sleepy to finish the game. Once again, Victoria was first in the bathroom. While James was in the bathroom, she unrolled the sleeping bags, unzipped them to lay flat. When He came out of the bathroom, she patted the bag beside herself. "I'd better sleep on the couch, Vicki, too hard for me to get up and down. Thanks anyway." In a few minutes he felt her come up on the couch with him. He smiled to himself and draped an arm around her waist, kissed her on the cheek "Goodnight, my Vicki" he said and he heard her murmur, sleepily "I love you, James" and they fell sound asleep.

They awoke early this morning. Both were hungry. They dressed and went into the kitchen. Vicki made coffee while James opened a can of meat. He sliced it while Victoria got the skillet and put a small pat of lard in the pan. James kept an eye on the meat while Vicki made more pancakes. When both the meat and the pancakes were done, they refilled their cups and sat down to their breakfast. It was OH, SO GOOD!

Today James wanted to try his skill with his crutch. They went out onto the porch and he asked Victoria to stand near as he tried to maneuver down the steps. There were three. James slowly placed his crutch onto the first step going down and hopped down with his good leg. Slowly he did the same again and once more and he was on the ground. "Let's go look around the Old Barn. I'll take my gun and my camera."

"Okay," replied Vicki, but I'm not going to paint now, so I'll just tag along with you—to keep you company, okay?"

"Good idea," said James. They walked, carefully out to the Old Barn and went inside the front door. It was a big barn. There were stalls that once held horses and a hayloft, but the back half of it had fallen in. There were old tools, hay rakes, an old tractor in a room off to the right side. Baling wire rolls left from when hay was stored there, even a small spool of barbwire, other odds and ends. They decided to walk to the spot that James had seen the coyote. As they neared, the piece of old cloth that the coyote slept on, Vicki stumbled and fell over a piece of something metal. She began to push aside the old cloth and debris and discovered a large metal door. James tried to pull it open, but with him hobbling on his crutch, this task he couldn't do. It was at this point that

Victoria remembered seeing a sledgehammer on their way here, so she told James to wait a minute and she ran to get the hammer. She drug and pulled it back to where he waited. She swung with all her might and hit the lock—it fell off. They both took hold of the door to pull it open and discovered that it slid on a track. As it opened completely, they saw a wide set of stairs with handrails. Can you manage, James? He nodded Yes. She walked down beside him, down thirteen steps, then there was another door, again with a lock. Victoria went back for the hammer. The lock broke easily. They slowly pushed the door and it swung inward. What kind of place was this? It was some sort of MILITARY installation. There were maps on the walls, Old-fashioned dial phones, tela-types, flags on their poles standing in corners. There was a section of cubicles (15) and each was about eight feet by eight feet, and each held a communication device machine. There was a bathroom for each of the large sections, that the place was divided into. There were bunks and a kitchen area. One section was a game room with table games and some kind of video game, intriguing Military game. The whole place was as if everyone had suddenly disappeared! There were some uniforms left hanging in a closet. There were large weapon cases that had been left with the doors open.

"What is this place?" asked Victoria.

"I'm not sure," answered James, "but it looks as if it was a headquarters, probably a secret one, or a tracking station, A spy station, something very important at one time. I guess it served its purpose. Probably once was full of Military men who lived and worked here. An important part of some F.B.I.—OR C.I.A.—Spy program."

"Why was it in the Old Barn?" asked Victoria.

"It was probably the last place anyone would suspect anything like this to be located or even ever found," said James.

"Well, we had better go on up and out of here, but first I'd like some photos of this place," and James began taking shots, some in every section, all the rooms. When he was finished, they closed the doors and stepped up into the Old Barn. Victoria had the strange sense that something was watching them. She slowly turned and looked around. At first she saw nothing, but as her eyes adjusted to the gloom—she saw him—a man who was dressed in an animal skin of some kind. He had scraggly hair and a beard. He was looking directly at them! When James saw the look on Vicki's face, he followed her gaze and froze in place. WHO was this and What did he want. HE stood a moment then turned and ran out the back of the barn and off into the woods.

James recovered first. "Did you see that, wasn't that a Man?"

"YES, SOME kind of Man! Where did he come from?"

"I just stepped out of the basement room and there he stood! He must stay around here somewhere—do you suppose he lives in the cabin?—or perhaps down in this Basement place? I saw no sign of anyone living down there, did you? Not a thing to indicate that someone LIVED THERE."

"No," said James, "maybe he lives out in the woods—maybe there's a cave somewhere near here. I don't believe he lives in the cabin."

"James, how long do you think the basement-room has been there?"

"For quite awhile I imagine—the phones and the tela-types and the radio communicators are from the 1960's at least, and the uniforms have changed somewhat from then to the present time. The refrigerator and store are from the seventies, I'd say," said James, "And I wonder HOW long it's been abandoned?"

"How long has this cabin been here, do you have any idea" asked Victoria. "Do you suppose all the buildings, the cabin, the barn, and the Military Station below—were all built at the same time—to camouflage the Station?"

"Well, let's go back to the cabin and Relax if we can, and think about this," said James, "I'll feel much better with a locked door between me and some strange men!"

When they got to the cabin, James set his camera on the small table in the living room and asked if Vicki would make them a cup of tea. They were both quite shaken at finding the Military Station, Or whatever it was, and then seeing the scraggly man. They discussed this for some length of time and still couldn't make any sense of anything of what they had seen.

"Do you suppose anyone else has ever discovered the STATION and does the man have anything to do with it?" asked Victoria.

"Maybe he was left to look after it," said James.

But why for so long—it's been there for, at least, thirty some-odd years, and only Heaven knows HOW long it's been vacant and just—just—there. "Maybe we'll go out tomorrow and look again. There should be an exit out somewhere, another way to enter and leave besides the sliding door. We'll look again tomorrow, ok, now just relax! I've used all of this film, so I'm going to take this out and reload. Can you put this used one in my backpack, Please. I will start afresh with a new film for tomorrow," he said. "How about a quick game of Dominoes, Vickie—I feel lucky tonight." He put the chairs near the small table and took the dominoes out and shuffled them. They played two games of dominoes and decided to read some before going to bed. They were sitting on the big old couch reading and that's where they both fell asleep for the night. Vicki woke up once when she thought she heard a soft footstep. She listened for a minute and when hearing nothing more, she stepped to look out the window. The moon was bright and there in the moonlight sat the coyote. He sniffed the air a few times and then loped off toward the barn. Victoria fell asleep again in a short time.

Both awoke to a bright morning and as usual—both were ready for breakfast as soon as their eyes were open—well, almost that fast! They got dressed quickly and Victoria went into the kitchen. Victoria opened a can of the meat, heated it and made little fried bread patties and coffee, of course.

"When we finish," said James, "we'll go back and look at the Station again. We will look for a back exit."

"Are you going to take more pictures of the Station? Before we leave here?" Victoria asked.

"Yes," said James, "I just refilled my camera—Where is my camera? I left it over on the other couch, did you move it?"

"No, I haven't seen it at all!" They looked all over and about the room, but no camera! Something sensed Vicki to look toward the door that opened to the stairway to the two bedrooms above. It was open—unlocked but not ajar. "James," she whispered, "the door is unlocked," she pointed to the door. "Did you open it?"

"He shook his head NO and picked up his gun. He went on cat feet to the door and threw it open. Nothing but stairs! He carefully started up the steps with Vicki right behind him. The stairway opened into a large room, a bedroom. There was a dresser, a bed, a small lamp table, but nothing more. Who had opened the door to the living room? and Why? There was a door across the bedroom and they advanced forward and pulled it open . . . A bathroom and adjoining that . . . another bedroom. They went back down into the living room.

"Let's go check the Station now, we'll find the camera later," said James. As they stepped from the porch and started for the barn—there on the ground lay James's camera. Vicki picked it up and handed it to him—he exclaimed, "The film has been removed. Why would someone remove brand-new film?" asked James.

"Maybe they thought it was the film you used yesterday down in the Station Room, maybe someone doesn't want pictures to be taken of the STATION ROOM, but WHY?—it's obviously been abandoned for many years. The only one we've seen is the griggled haired, bearded one. It must have been him—who else is there to do it?" asked Victoria, "BUT WHY?"

They had reached the barn by now and went directly to the sliding door. They entered at the door at the bottom of the wide stairs. They moved slowly and cautiously—maybe the grizzly man was down here. Did he live here? Once again they entered the room with all the communication devices. From here on into the Bunk

Room—or barrack. There were double bunks, one above the other, all along the sides of the room. There was a large room with a row of showers next to the barrack room. Other rooms followed some with other apparatus in them and then into the kitchen which held several long dining tables of metal. There was a large pantry with cans of foods, then a laundry room, washers and dryers from the seventies. Even a couple of ironing boards were spotted. At the back of a hall that came from the laundry room, was another metal door. James pulled it open and *there* was a round silo-like room with a ladder going up.

"Do you want to climb it Victoria . . . and see where it leads? I can't do it myself," said James.

"Can I borrow your gun?" she asked.

"Of course," he replied, and with the gun in her pocket, she started up the ladder. It went straight up for about ten feet and stopped at the beginning of a tunnel that went farther out. The space in the tunnel was about five feet high so Vicki had to stoop to get through. It stopped abruptly in a small round room, with another ladder that led to a trap door. Once more she climbed the ladder and pushed the top open. She climbed out and got the surprise of her life! She was standing inside a well. Not a real well, but when the trap door was closed, it was made to resemble a "FILLED WITH DEBRIS" old well. ?? few ladder rungs and Victoria stepped out onto the ground. She was out behind the Old barn about three hundred feet among a few trees. So THIS was the Exit! She went back the way she had come to where James waited for her.

"Well," he asked, "Where does it go?"

"At the top of this ladder there's a tunnel which leads to a small room with a trapdoor above. Open the trap door and you're in a FAKE well that is filled with fake debris. It ends about three hundred feet behind the barn, among a few trees. The well isn't really a well, but a silo. It's the exit to the STATION.

Well, let's go back thru the STATION and see if we've missed anything. They started back thru the STATION and as they neared the bunkroom, they heard a noise and out from a section of the floor that opened—was MR. SCRAGGLY MAN. He saw them and started back down, but Vicki had drawn the gun from her pocket and said "I don't know how long you've been here—but it won't be any longer if you don't come up here—NOW!"

He slowly came out and put his hands up high.

"WHO are You and what are you doing Here?"

"I give up," he said, "you've found me after thirty years. I've never told anyone about what happened here, but I know you are from the F.B.I. or C.I.A. as you guys are called now and I knew you would never give up, that you'd come for me someday, so here I am."

"What are you talking about, Mr.? We aren't F.B.I. or anyone like that. I'm a photographer and Victoria owns a Shoe Business and she paints. Why do you think that we are after you?" asked James.

"I knew you would find me someday. I'm not afraid to die, go ahead and shoot me, I'm tired—I've been hiding for thirty years now."

"But WHY?" asked James. "You come on to the cabin and we'll have a cup of tea and you can tell us your story."

When they were seated and had their cups of tea, he said "my name is Daniel Lyons and I witnessed something that no one was supposed to see."

"Maybe you'd better tell us the whole story—from the beginning to the end. Does it have to do with this Military Installation?" asked James.

He nodded his head yes, and he began;—"It was in nineteen seventy five, a few of us, actually there were six of us, I was the youngest, twenty-two. We were all friends, some of us like brothers. We decided to go hunting in an OFF-Limit place, a nature reserve. We planned to fly in under the radar, spend the day hunting and fly back out. We all knew this was an illegal thing to do, so we made no flight plan with the authorities. We had a few beers on the way up to the far side of this mountain, on the other side of the deep canyon behind here. This is, we were kind of a wild bunch of young men. Somehow our pilot didn't figure his plan too well and we ran out of fuel. Doc had to set the plane down. We were desperately looking for somewhere he could put the plane down—glide in. That's when we spotted the grassy place of the hill behind here, before the second and third and final place to put it down before the drop off of the canyon rim. Doc glided in—made a pretty good landing but a rough and scary one—too close to the rim of the canyon. We were all pretty well shook up. When we stopped, Doc tried to reach someone on the radio, but somehow we had lost our frequency. So me being the youngest, Doc told me to climb up to the highest point of the hill and see if I could reach anyone on the radio, the hand one. All of them got out with their rifle sand began to walk forward. I made it to the high point and turned back to see where the boys went. I had just sat down for a cigarette and I saw the boys climbing up the grassy hill. They were too far for my naked eye to see, so I looked thru the scope of my rifle. They were almost to the barn when I saw them start to run back toward the plane. It was then I saw why they were running. A small group of Military stood just out behind the barn, rifles raised and one by one my friends were shot. I couldn't believe my eyes! Why was our own ?? Military shooting and killing my friends. I watched in horror as they were piled into a wagon and taken down to the plane and a military detail dug graves for all of them together. Then they pushed the plane down to the low part near the rim and they all gave it a push and it rolled down and over the rim of the canyon and fell crashing again and again against the walls of the canyon until it was just a pile of metal laying at the bottom of the canyon. I was sick to my stomach and scared to death! THEY MUST NEVER FINE ME! For weeks they looked to see if there was anyone else. They guarded the road that comes up back—in fact they put up a sign at the bottom of the hill that said the road was closed and dangerous. I hid in a cave, a strange cave which was reached from up above, so it was a pretty safe place. I ate rabbit and fowls, even a snake every now and then. I was determined to find out who these men were in those Military uniforms and WHAT they were doing here, way off in the mountains—remote mountains. One night I dared to come down and look around. There were no guards posted anywhere in sight. After they put up the closed sign at the bottom of the hill, I never saw any guards. I found the WELL (silo) one night and made my way into the Compound. Everyone was busy on the machines and scopes, telatypes, etc. communicating with people allover the world. I never did find out exactly what the place was for, but I kept out of sight. There's a back door to the cabin and I slept there once in awhile. I didn't dare get caught because I knew exactly what my fate would be. The Military men stayed mostly inside the compound. There were two leaders who kept a close lookout. A helicopter brought supplies in every three months. Books, paper for the machines, some kind of lubricant for them also, and once or twice a year ammunition. I watched them unload on the grassy spot where my friends lay buried. Then one day, about two years after we had come, they all, one day, suddenly left! Loaded into the helicopters and were gone. I remained in hiding for a few more months and then I came to live here in the abandoned barn and eventually into the Compound itself. I keep thinking they will send someone to kill me if I show myself or tell anyone. I'm so afraid of what they would do if they knew what I saw. So, here I am. No one has ever talked to me, nor seen me until now. When you took the pictures, I knew you had come for me—or the government had sent the F.B.I. or the C.I.A. or someone to find me and kill me."

James asked, "Why have you never just walked out? Left and gone home?"

"Well, look at it from my point of view—all my best friends were gone, and I thought IF I went home with this tale of them being killed by our Military—Well, their families would want me to tell the story and I knew if I did—they would find and kill me. I have witnessed something that no one was ever to know. So I just stayed here. I've become used to being alone, except for Charley, the coyote. He lives in the barn. So, what are you going to do to me," he asked.

"We are not going to do anything to you. We are waiting another day and then Victoria will go bring the jeep for me. You can do whatever you want to do—you're free—no one is looking for you. They don't know you exist. When they killed your friends, they didn't see you—they never knew you existed."

The next morning early, Victoria went back to James' cabin and drove the jeep up the rutty old road, she was so thankful that she brought the jeep. She picked James up and they were going, but at that moment, the old man said "Well since the cabin and barn were built to camouflage the Compound and its been deserted for all these years, I think I'll homestead it and make the compound into suites for summer rentals. I'll live in the Old Cabin and live here forever. I will call myself Daniel Lyons. You two can come back once in awhile." s they drove off Old Daniel smiled to himself. He was remembering how he had picked the Military men off, one at a time, until they were all gone. Just as he had done to his five friends who had helped steal the one million and eight hundred thousand which now was his. Not only did the plane lay at the bottom of the deep canyon, but so did the ashes of his five friends and the fifteen military men who had lived beneath the barn—and a few curious others who chanced upon Old Daniel—in his lyon's Den.

The End

By Dimmon

STANLLEY'S GHOST
OF
CHATEAU LE FLUER

Stanley, a real ESTATE man, is selling the OLD CHATEAU LE FLUER to a MR. LOMBARDO (PETE), a jeweler who doesn't know that the HOUSE is rumored to be haunted.

Stanley who has seen the ghost himself, is deciding whether to tell Mr. Lombardo that the house is "rumored" to be haunted.

According to Stanley's MOTHER, THIS ISN'T HIS FIRST Encounter with a ghost.

"Stanley's Ghost"

Stanley was a nice man. Well mannered, mild temperament and a happy-appearanced man. He went to work everyday, he went to Church on Sunday, gave his tithes faithfully, tipped his hat to ladies, gave them the seat on the streetcar and bus, opened doors for them and never swore in their company! He visited his old Mother once a week and had breakfast. He went shopping for her when she was Under The Weather OR took her If she was feeling well.

He had one sister who lived two states away, who came Once a year to Visit Mama for a week. She, Cloe, was a big executive in a large housing development. She was always busy! If he called her on the phone, she could only speak for a minute or two—she was due at a meeting or Whatever? She had been married once but was too aggressive for him—or—any man! She lived in a four bedroom condo that she had bought a few years ago, but she was always re-doing, up-dating it. It WAS a beautiful lace upon a small hill not far too the beach.

Stanley lived in a two bedroom Spanish-style house with a red-tiled roof. His yard was full of flowers and plants, especially his front yard! His backyard had a patio with a fireplace, a place to cook and a pool—a lovely kidney shaped pool. He didn't entertain often, but when he did, everyone had a wonderful time! Stanley was an AWESOME Host! He always had plenty of food and drinks and not all were alcoholic.

If someone did happen to drink too much, was unable to drive home—there was always a place to spend the night. Although Stanley had only one Actual guest bedroom, he had his "Sun room." It had been his back porch and Stanley had it converted into his Sunroom—and in this sunroom was an extra place to sleep. Stanley was proud of his house and yards. He drove a new car, a Honda. Stanley owned a Real ESTATE Company. He was very thrifty, watched his monies carefully.

Stanley had no Special Lady but he had a couple of good friends he could depend on should he need a partner for any reason. There was Sheryl who had been married twice, but had no one right now. She was a modest nice lady. If he needed a lady to go with him to some of his meetings, she was the one he chose. He had taken her on some of his conventions. She had her own room, but the rest of the time she was with Stanley.

Now, Gloria was another story! If he ever (and he sometimes did) feel like kicking up his heels and over the traces—Gloria was his choice. She loved to dance and if she had a couple of drinks too many, she was ready for SEX and Gloria knew all about how to please a man, even one like Stanley! Gloria knew that once she got him started, it was an all night thing. Stanley had his ways like no other man she had ever known, and she had *known* quite a few!

Of course Sheryl and Stanley had Sex—once and Sheryl had to rest for a couple of days. Stanley's actions scared her a little. She always made sure she had her own room when she went to conventions with him!

Stanley had this one big place up in the foothills, that he had been trying to get rid of for the last year. Today he was going to show it to a Mr. Lombardo who said that he dealt in jewelry—diamonds, rubies, emeralds, etc.

Stanley was reasonably sure that he would take it. Stanley's price for it was Cool Million Dollars. He was to meet him at ten a.m. on Wednesday, up at the HILL HOUSE as it was called.

It wasn't because it was up in the hills that it was called that. A Mr. Levi Hill had owned the place—had it built for his wife ANNE, his Lady Anne, his lifetime love. BUT, somehow love turned sour and she was found dead at the bottom of the stairs. No, she hadn't fallen and no one pushed her. She had a gunshot in her back—directly into her heart. She died quickly. When the police got there (Levi had called them) they found him sitting beside her holding one of her hands. Mr. Hill had been in prison now for twenty-five years. He had gotten Life Without Parole. They had no children. The house stood empty for several years. No one wanted a Haunted House. It was said that her ghost roamed sometimes at night. NOW, even IF you're NOT a big believer in ghosts, It's hard to live in a house that is *Believed* to be haunted with a ghost!

Finally after it sat empty (maybe the ghost was there but there was no one to see her) for about eight years, then a Mr. Danbury bought it and a Makeover Changed some room's dimensions, made arches where doors once were. Added some details to the ceiling and redid the stairways big banister. Added a small breakfast room from a ONCE SMALL Entryway. The house ended up more European looking. Then Mr. Danbury sold it to a Mr. Lemmon, a man from France. He had a wife and two teenage children. When his children went away to college, he and his wife sold it and went back to France.

Stanley was the realtor who was handling the sale of Chateau DeFluer, once known as Hill House.

When Stanley drove up in his Honda there was a B.M.W. in the circular driveway. Mr. Lombardo was sitting on the bench on the small front porch. He stood and offered his hand to Stanley. "Great looking house from the outside, anyway. I love the circular drive. How old is this house?"

It was built in 1964, but it's been completely Refurbished by a Mr. Danbury. He sold it to a Mr. and Mrs. Lemmon from France but he and his wife decided to go back to France about a year ago and they are selling it. There are only three who have owned it since it was built." Stanley unlocked the door and they entered into the Great Room with the long, sweeping stairway. "Wow, What a house!" said Mr. Lombardo, "just what I need for entertaining my business associates," he said. Wait until they get a load of this! He's rather rough around the edges, Stanley thought to himself, but he must have money from Somewhere—he knows the price of the house.

"I'd like to see the kitchen, Mr. Lombardo said next. A man who likes to eat needs a great kitchen! Again Stanley detected a touch of crudeness in his speech.

"Now for the bedrooms," said Lombardo, "one doesn't always sleep in the same bedroom—there may be a couple of t hem you want to try in the same night—you may have Company who requires one's services, right Stanley?"

Stanley was beginning to have second thoughts about even selling this great house to much an uncouth sounding man, But he needed to see it. He could use his commission, his bank account had dwindled some. He had to help pay for his mother's medicine for a few months now. He and Cloe both, helped with her medicines. So, Stanley tried to ignore Mr. Lombardo's remarks. They finished looking at the remainder of the house. Mr. Lombardo said he'd call Stanley on Friday with his decision—but he was fairly certain, he would buy it. Mr. Lombardo drove away.

Stanley went back in to lock the backdoor and as he turned around—there she stood at the bottom of the stairs. She was a beautiful woman—a ghost. She smiled at him and walked away toward the kitchen. The closer to the kitchen she got, the more transparent she became until she was no longer there.

Stanley was totally shocked! He was speechless! He was sure he had seen her, but why would she appear to him? He had seen a picture of her once in the Newspaper at the Library just after she had died. There was NO doubt, He had seen LADY ANNE!

Stanley hadn't mentioned Chateau DeFluer being haunted, frankly because Stanley had never REALLY believed in ghosts. Should he say anything to Mr. Lombardo? or not? Would it matter to him? He seemed to be a rather ignorant man so maybe he was superstitious about many things, and wouldn't buy the place. In the end Stanley stayed quiet about the house being haunted.

On the Wednesday before the Friday that he was to buy the house, Mr. Lombardo called Stanley saying that he wanted new drapes. He would pay for them, but he needed the measurements of the Great Rooms windows. Now ordinarily Stanley would have had this done by professionals, but he decided to go out there and do the measuring himself—*and* have another look. Maybe he imagined the ghost? Anyway he drove out to the Chateau. He opened the door and walked into the room. It was just as he had left it. He brought the ladder from the storage shed, climbed up with his measuring tape. He measured the two lower ones about eight feet high and had climbed up to measure the TALL windows. He had measured one when all of a sudden he smelled perfume, potent perfume. He felt his ladder move slightly and glanced down, and there on the bottom rung stood Lady Anne smiling up at him. He almost lost his grip on the ladder so he made a grab for it. When he looked down again she was nowhere in sight. He slowly exited the ladder. He glanced around, but she was gone. He took the ladder back to the shed and as he crossed the patio next to the pool, there she was in the pool. Again she smiled and disappeared. Stanley had all he could handle of Lady Anne. He left quickly locking the door and drove away as fast as was legal.

Why was he seeing Lady Anne? Why was she smiling that MONA LISA smile at him? He found the whole thing alarming and a little frightening.

The next evening he called and ask Sheryl out to dinner at the CAFE ELDARDO, a nice place that Sheryl liked. They ordered their wine and their dinner. The wine came first, of course, and they sat chit-chatting, and sipping their wine.

"What have you been up to for the lat few days?" asked Sheryl.

"Well, as you know I've been wanting to sell HILL HOUSE OR Chateau DeFluer as it's now called. I have a Mr. Lombardo I'm hoping will buy it—he wants it but there's a few things he wanted done first. I need your advice on something, Sheryl. The old house is said to be haunted by Lady Anne who was killed there by her husband, Levi Hill about thirty-three years ago. Some people claim to have seen her over those years. Should this be mentioned to Mr. Lombardo?"

"Oh, Stanley, you've got to be kidding! That was a long time ago and most people don't *Really* believe in ghosts. You've been trying to sell that place, if I were you, I'd keep my mouth shut and sell the house. How long has it been since anyone has mentioned a ghost there?"

Mr. Danbury bought it and had it changed, somewhat and some of the workers say they saw her while they were working there. One worker who decided to finish a door before he left and about Eight O'clock, said that she came and stood beside him. He swore this! He would never work late again and neither would anyone else after he told this. I haven't heard anyone say anything lately.

"Oh! Stanley you've shown the place now for about a year and IF she were there I'm sure you would have seen her—just sell the house, Stanley and forget about ghosts—that's my advice to you." Their food arrived at that moment and the conversation was silenced for awhile. Stanley took her home and she ask if he wanted to come in for awhile and talk. He thanked her, but no, he would take a rain check as he was tired tonight. He was Much tireder when morning came—he had stopped for a drink with Gloria and he was OH, so tired—but Very Pleased; and happy. Gloria had that effect on Stanley.

He slept until noon, decided to go by Mama's and have lunch with her. He picked something up on the way there. She was so pleased to see him. As they had their lunch, Stanley told her about Mr. Lombardo buying the old HILL HOUSE and he said to her "Mama, do you remember there was some talk of it being haunted by Lady Anne's ghost?" Mama nodded. "Do you think I should mention this to Mr. Lombardo?"

"Well, said Mama, I think since you've been trying to sell it for a year now and someone Finally wants it—I'd just keep my mouth shut for now. *If* he happens to see the ghost, since he will now own the house, it will be HIS ghost and he will have to decide what he wants to do with it. Is this a malicious ghost? Has she hurt anyone?"

"I've never heard of anything like that," Mama.

"Then go ahead and sell the house to him."

"Thank you, Mama," he said as he kissed her cheek and ask "Have you ever seen a ghost, Mama?"

She turned and looked directly at him into his eyes and said "Yes, I have, Stanley, once long ago when you were about two years old. You were in your room playing with a ball. I heard you laughing and I went to see why you were laughing. There I found a young woman of about twenty years of age, playing ball with you. You rolled it to her and she rolled it back to you. When she saw me she was gone in one "Poof. You cried when she disappeared. She came one more time—when you were ill. Your temperature was high so I had been sitting beside your bed and I fell asleep. I awoke suddenly to find her standing beside your bed crying. I never saw her again but I would hear you laughing and no one was there, that I ever saw. I always thought you were one of those special people who have a connection with the Spirit World, Stanley. Maybe this is why you feel that perhaps you should mention that you've heard that it is haunted. I don't think you will ever be afraid of ghosts, Stanley, since you've already seen one and played ball with her. But don't you remember that I went to the library to see if there had ever been a tragedy there. And found out that there was a house there before, that burned down, and a small boy had burned to death in it."

Stanley heard this story with an open mind. Mama was old now and probably saw a movie and thought it was real. She sometimes got the real and things muddled. "Mama, I'm going now. I have to get a carpet changed at HILL HOUSE. Mr. Lombardo doesn't like the color of the one in the Library. I have the carpet men coming at Two-thirty and I must stop for gas. Be a good girl, take care, listen to the nurse and you know how much I LOVE you, Mama" and he kissed the top of her head. Mama's story bothered him some because he was scared of ghosts! How do you tell if a ghost is good OR bad?

When he got to Hill House the delivery truck was waiting. He unlocked the door, turned the light and the fan on to cool the place off.

They had brought a really beautiful carpet an improvement over the original one. The men went right to work taking out the old and placing the new. While they were doing this, Stanley went upstairs to the Master Bedroom. A wonderfully big and high ceilinged room. It held a large king size bed in mahogany, a dresser, a chest and two tables to be used as nightstands. There was a desk of the same wood. It had a peri-winkle blue carpet and drapes. Not exactly a man's color, thought Stanley, but a nice room. He walked over to the bedroom window and looked out. What was a van doing in the alleyway behind the house? He could see two men inside and one looked like Mr. Lombardo! What were they dong? They were unloading boxes and putting them in the Pool House! How did they get the keys to the Pool House? and what were they unloading? Just as soon as they left, he would go find out just WHAT was stored in the Pool House.

After the carpet men had gone, Stanley went to see what had been put in there.

Now, what even Mr. Lombardo or Mr. Lemmon didn't know, was that beneath the back entry floor was an old wine cellar with a passage way into the Pool House. Stanley had found it long ago, quite by accident, and never mentioned it to anyone. He now took this route to the pool house. When he got inside, there were many boxes of many sizes. What in Heaven's name was in these boxes? He found one that had a loose flap and pulled it open. What was this? Jewelry of all kinds; brooches, earrings, bracelets, rings—all kind of jewelry. Were all of these boxes (twelve in all) full of jewelry? Mr. Lombardo had said that he was a jeweler, but these boxes were from several different countries. Were these the ones he was going to sell in his store? Did he even have a store? This was a lot of jewelry, enough for two stores! This wasn't the best place to store them! Why didn't he ask and put them inside the Chateau? Something was not Kosher here—Stanley could feel it in his bones—something about Mr. Lombardo was AMISS.

On Friday Mr. Lombardo sealed the deal for Chateau DeFluer. Stanley was glad to have this deal over and done with. The ghost was Mr. Lombardo's problem now.

About two weeks later he got a note from Mr. Lombardo asking him to a House Warming Party at the Chateau on Saturday night. Bring your own lady—I've got the booze! Stanley stood still looking at the note and thinking "Do I really want to go to Mr. Lombardo's house-warming party?" Who would he take and WHAT could he take for a gift to a man like Lombardo? with all the jewelry he had seen in the pool house, what could Mr. Lombardo want? After a couple of days of deciding if he wanted to take Sheryl or Gloria, he ask Gloria if she would like to go and of course she said yes. So now all he had to do was find a gift for Mr. Lombardo!

For the next two days he hunted for a gift but came up empty handed.

On Saturday, he took Sheryl to lunch at the RED DRAGON Chinese restaurant downtown. After their lunch as they were walking back to his car, they passed a small, dingy-looking, old antique shop. As they reached the display window, Sheryl exclaimed "Oh, Stanley look! What a beautiful old antique brooch. I want to go in and look at it." They entered and Sheryl ask to see the Brooch in the window. While the owner retrieved it from the window, Stanley was browsing around looking at all the things an antique store has, when way down in one corner of a case, he spotted a crystal and onyx dragon. He had jade eyes and onyx claws and the tips of the scales of his tail were onyx. He was a Great Dragon! Perfect for Mr. Lombardo's Party. Stanley asked how much for the dragon?

"Well," said the owner, "He's been here for a long time! He was already here when I bought the store twenty years ago. He's an old one. I'll take $250 for him. He's worth a lot more, but dragons aren't as popular as they once were, too many Science fiction movies have ruined their charm. Do you want him?" Stanley knew it was a great dragon, an outstanding dragon, even a gift. A little more than he really wanted to pay—but it was the perfect gift! So Stanley bought him. Sheryl offered to take him home, clean him up and have him gift-wrapped for Stanley. He thanked her *and* bought the sapphire and ruby brooch for her.

The following Saturday found Stanley in his best suit, peach shirt and grey tie. He looked very handsome, Gloria told him when he picked her up. She wore a peach Halter dress with a small floral wreath on her hair. Her shoes were nothing but straps and a sole. She was a woman who could hold her own wherever she was taken. She was a charming conversationalist, on many subjects.

When they arrived there was quite a crowd already. As they entered Mr. Lombardo was talking to two men: one was tall and elegantly dressed with a handsome face. The other one was tall also but not as tall as the first man, and he wasn't elegant! He wore a strange expression—almost a sneer. Mr. Lombardo left them and came to greet Stanley and Gloria. "Gloria this is our host, Mr. Lombardo, and this is Gloria." He shook her hand commented on how lovely she looked. Gloria, always being in charge of herself in all situations Thanked him with a nod of her head and a Thank You. They then went to place their gift with the rest of them. They said HELLO and introduced themselves to whomever spoke to them. In a short time they had met half, at least, of most of the people in the room. They then wandered over for a drink and were told to help themselves to any of refreshments they wanted. Stanley had wandered away and was looking at the long staircase—and there stood Lady Anne in her party attire. She once again smiled at him, took a few steps down the stairs and as before, she vanished. Stanley quickly turned around to see if anyone had seen her. Apparently no one had! Gloria was having a conversation with the tall handsome man who was smiling down at Gloria. She must have said something witty because he tossed his head back and laughed. At this moment Mr. Lombardo up and said to Stanley "I want to talk to you about a few things. How about you come out on Monday about ten-A.M. It's about the house."

"Okay," said Stanley. He and Gloria left about midnight, no gifts had been opened yet. He drove Gloria to her house where he spent the rest of the night in their usual way—and there was little sleeping!

They awoke about noon, showered and went to the kitchen where Gloria made a delicious breakfast. She was good in the kitchen, too!—thought Stanley to himself.

Today was Sunday and Mama wanted to go to church. Stanley put on his blue suit and went to pick up Mama. She was ready when he got there and the nurse had Mama looking very pretty. They sat on the third row from the front and Mama AMENED when she thought it appropriate to do so. She spoke to the people she knew and some she introduced herself to. She smiled and GOD BLESSED them all and Stanley was glad he had brought her.

"Where do you want to eat lunch today, Mama?"

"How about if we drive out to the lake to the restaurant there, and have a nice fish luncheon, Stanley. How does that sound," asked Mama"

"Just fine, Mama, a good idea." So out to the lake Stanley drove. The luncheon was wonderful and his Mama was feeling fine today, so Stanley was a contented man. They even had dessert; apple pie with ice-cream—Mama's favorite. They had a great day together. They stopped by the pharmacy on the way home and he stopped to pick up Mama's medicine. He then took Mama home where she promptly fell asleep in her big old chair. He kissed the top of her head and left. He Loved his Mama!

On Monday at ten A.M. he rang the bell at the Chateau DeFluer. It was answered by some guy who took Stanley into the kitchen where Mr. Lombardo was having coffee. He offered him a cup and he sat down at the table with Mr. Lombardo, who waited until his man was gone, then he looked at Stanley and said "There's something strange about this house, Stanley, things are moved around from place to place. I left my wallet by my bed one night and I found it on the mantle of the fireplace downstairs. Sometimes my clothes are removed from my room and the shower comes on by itself and there's no one there. What is the explanation for this? Do you have any idea? Do I have a ghost in this house or is someone hiding out here? Is this house haunted?

"Well, really, I don't know what goes on in this house. *I've* never lived here or spent a night. How would I know anything? Have you ask your people—your maids about it?"

"NO—I haven't—yet. I don't want them to think I'm nuts. I'm a BIG jewelry dealer, I don't want the people I deal with to think I'm incompetent!"

"Have any of them seen anything OR mentioned anything about 'THINGS' being moved?" asked Stanley.

"No—no one has said anything—except a coupe of days ago, the kitchen maid as *if I'd* put the fire under the tea kettle. And a guest of mine who spent a few days here ask me WHO played games in the pool house? Seems she saw a woman there reading a book. One of my men went to start the car and his keys went flying as if they had been thrown. Of course the other man with him, just laughed at him being clumsy. So you see, I have reason to think that this place IS STRANGE."

"Well, just keep your eyes open and keep me posted, said Stanley and call if you find out who is playing these tricks on you." As Stanley stood to go—there she stood in her apron with a very satisfied smirk on her face. He frowned at her and "POOF" she was gone.

"What are you frowning at Stanley?"

"I was just looking at the stove and thinking about the fire being lit under the tea kettle. Well, so long, I must be going. I have another appointment in town." What was he to do about Mr. Lombardo's ghost?

About a month later, Mr. Lombardo called and said to Stanley, "I think I may have to leave the Chateau and put it up for sale. Something or someone is taking my jewelry. Some of it has disappeared. I've checked with all my men and NO ONE knows anything about it. I've had them watched closely and they haven't been near the jewelry, which by-the-way-is in my room, so I'd know if it was one of them."

"Why don't you set-up a camera in there and see IF you can catch anyone, Mr. Lombardo?" suggested Stanley.

"GREAT IDEA," said Mr. Lombardo. I should have thought of that! Thanks, Stanley."

About a week after this, a very shaky voiced Lombardo called and said "COME out HERE QUICKLY—I have something to show you! When Stanley arrived, a disheveled Lombardo answered the door. "Come on up," he said, as he lead the way to his bedroom. "Look at this, Stanley," as he turned on the camera. At first the room was still and quiet. Then they saw one of the boxes open and pieces of jewelry was taken out, one piece at a time, BUT there was no one there! The pieces moved out of view into Mr. Lombardo's room. "See," he said, "the jewelry moves out by itself. How can that be?" But Stanley saw what Mr. Lombardo could not see. There was Lady ANNE taking what she wanted of Mr. Lombardo's jewels. "You see, it leaves by itself—But Where does it Go?" The camera only covers this room. Stanley thought he knew where it was, but he wasn't going to expose the secret room beneath the mud room entry with its hallway to the pool house. No one knew about it, so Stanley was quiet. If Mr. Lombardo wanted to put the Chateau up for sale, He—Stanley would handle it for him.

Mr. Lombardo moved out within three days. His men packed all the boxes back into the truck and they ALL were gone. Gone back to VESASA. He wanted only what he'd paid for it—a million dollars and once again Stanley was to handle the sale.

Stanley sent a clean-up crew to the Chateau and they were there for a couple of days; polishing the floors, cleaning the drapes and the carpet.

The day after they were all finished, Stanley went to the Chateau one evening. He went into the room beneath the floor and there he found the jewelry; a ruby ring, a diamond necklace, with matching earrings, A sapphire brooch and a jade ring . . . . and What was This?—The beautiful Crystal Dragon that he had given Mr. Lombardo? He put all these things in a bag and went up to the room that had been Mr. Lombardo's bedroom where he had seen an attaché case of leather. It was still there on a shelf of the closet. He took it down and emptied the things from the bag to the attaché case. When he had finished, he dusted himself off, picked up the case and walked to the bedroom door—and there stood Lady Anne. She held out her hand YOU don't frighten me, Lady Anne . . . I've seen ghosts before! She held out her hand again and this time there was no smile. He tried to pass by her, but she stepped in front of him again holding out her hand and this time was Anger in her eyes. He tried to pass her once again but she moved to the side and faced him. He quickly darted past her and laughed, as he made a run for the stairs. He glanced around to see her as he reached the stairs . . . she wasn't there, but as he took the top step—there she was in front of him and he felt himself down, down and his attaché case fell, spilling out all the jewels which went tumbling down, down to the bottom of the stairs. As he hit the floor at the bottom and knew he had seen his last day of life, he saw her wicked smile as she bent to retrieve her jewelry. As his eyes closed in death, he said "God forgive me and take care of MY Mama."

THEY found him two days later. Sheryl had called the police to check the Chateau. His death was pronounced as accidental. It seemed he had stumbled on an item on the stairs . . . . A crystal dragon with jade eyes and onyx claws and onyx dipped scale-tips! His friends and family were devastated. Such A good man! What an awful way to go! They would miss him terribly!

The Chateau was there for many years to come. Several people bought it . . . but sold it just as quickly. Everyone remarked on what a beautiful place it was! But by and by it got the title HAUNTED and no one wanted it and eventually there was only one presence there (or was there), THE Lady ANNE for whom it had been built.

IT was told by some—that late in the evening when all was still, she could be seen on the terrace, in her party dress with her jewels, and once in awhile she was dancing with a man with a handsome man holding a Crystal jade ????????????????????? Dragon.

THE BIKER'S DISCOVERY

Mitchell was in VIETNAM for six years and it changed him: his outlook of the world. HE was and IS a Good man, a biker! He got his first bike, A Old Indian, when he was sixteen, and he was hooked!

HE bought A HOG WHEN HE GOT HOME from NAM.

On a trip thru Nevada, Utah, Wyoming and Colorado, he finds the woman of his dreams. HE'S been looking for her for almost thirty years, BUT—can he LEGALLY HAVE her?

"The Biker's Surprise"

Mitchell loved his Bike. He had ridden a BIKE since he was sixteen, his first one, that is. It was given to him by an old Uncle who never rode it anymore after his last accident. It was an Old INDIAN and he'd had to FIX it before he could ride it, but he did with the help of his Uncle Ray. Uncle Ray died a couple of years later from a complication from one of those Long-age accidents of his old BIKE RIDING days.

Mitchell went into the Marines at the age of seventeen and a half, right out of High School. He left his BIKE with a neighbor across the street.

Well, Mitchell's four years turned into six that he spent in Vietnam. BUT when he returned home with money in his pocket from the government and his Extra he'd won from his Marine buddies, he bought himself a new Harley HOG. His old Indian he gave to the son of the neighbor who had kept his Bike for him.

Mitchell really loved his New Hog and he knew that IF his Mama was alive would say he SINNED by gambling for his HOG.

Mitchell wasn't a bad guy—he helped those who needed help, who were down and Out—he was a good neighbor and he was Half-Way gentleman when ladies were around. He liked women IN Their Own Place, but not the bossy type, and *especially* one who was a BOSS Of a crew of men. Women had no place at all, in his opinion, to be a BOSS of men! He had seen too much of that bossiness in h is neighbor, Walter's wife—Mildred! Walter was a HEN-PECKED man.

Walter worked everyday, rain, shine, sleet, or now—building homes and business complexes. He was a Field Supervisor.

Mildred was lazy, fat, and a bossy woman. The house was never clean, picked-up or tidy, Toys all over, clothes and towels left on the floor in the bathroom and ALWAYS a dirty sink area!

There was never any warm supper waiting for Walter. He even had to wash a dish before he could eat his Macaroni and Cheese or his frozen dinner, Which He himself had to make! He usually held one of the kids on his lap while he ate his dinner. Then he helped bathe the kids and put them to bed—while Mildred—rested!

Walter never had a day of fishing, ballgame, or playing pool with the boys. NO, poor Walter had a BOSS whom he listened to and—OBEYED!

Mitchell knew that IF Mildred and his wife—But she wouldn't be—because If she were: Mitchell would have taken her for a ride on the back of his Bike and she would have ACCIDENTALLY, as Mitchell raced suddenly around a curve, fallen off and over the edge of some wonderful, curvy road!

So Mitchell had decided to lave the Bossy women alone!

When he had first came back from Nam, he had worked for awhile for a company that built parts for the Oil Industry. The Boss of his area was a woman named Louise—who had less brains and more balls than he did. She made the mistake one day of ordering him to bring her a cup of coffee, HE told her he was busy overseeing the loading of a cargo shipment, which *was his* job.

Louise got right up in his face and said "If I tell you to bring me a cup of coffee Or a roll of toilet tissue—you'd Better Do It. I'm one of your bosses!

Mitchell looked coolly at her and said "Not for long—you're not. He took her to court and sued on Harassment charges (sexual). He won his case. She lost her job and FACE with the men, who cheered as she walked out. Then one day we said to himself "Remember when you were out there in those deep Jungles—you told yourself that IF you lived thru this mess, you would enjoy your freedom. So, what are you doing with your nose to the GRINDSTONE? Get on your Bike and ride freely and see more of this AMERICA that you fought so hard for out there in that Hell-hole jungle. You have no one but yourself to be responsible for. Go and Explore! and that's exactly what Mitchell did!

He took his bedroll, a slicker and his maps in one of his saddlebags. The other one held two changes of clothes, his toothbrush and his toiletries, small size—he would replenish when needed.

He left from his own state in early Spring. His state had many beautiful and interesting places and things to see, And he had, Some said that his state had some of what every other state had. He decided to go see the states up north. He wanted to see Utah, Wyoming and Colorado, at least some of each. He rode on thru the mountains on Beautiful scenic roads, not the State Highways, but the Biker's trails. These may be a little too curvy and deep canyoned for most travelers BUT BIKER's live for these routes! By the time he reached Reno, Nevada, he was ready for a sit-down meal and cold drink. I'll say here, that Mitchell wasn't a big drinker nor had he ever taken drugs. He never even had a beer and got right back on his BIKE. IF he had a beer, he waited at the place he had drunk it until he knew he was legal to drive again. This wasn't strictly because of the Law, Mitchell had seen the results of BEER and BIKES. He had seen enough death and waste of life in Nam, for a lifetime!

After eating, he went into one of the Casinos and stood at the Crap Table just watching for a few minutes. He knew he could possibly beat most of the players sitting around the table, so he put his money down. He lost the first hand, but placed his money again on the table. This time he won—not a lot, but enough for a few tanks of fuel for his trip. He had watched the men playing and found their tell-tell signs of a good hand; a raised brow, a flicker of the eye, a tiny smile around the mouth, etc., so he had won most of the hands, when a Willowy Blond dressed in her Western Style—strode up and laid her monies down. Mitchell watched her for any sign of "give away," but her face was set in stone, no flicker, no brow raise, no smile—nothing! Cool as a cucumber! Mitchell took his chips to the Banker and collected his cash, got on his Bike and rode out of RENO on Highway Eighty for awhile until he found the Bike route he wanted. It was a narrow, curvy road that ran along beside a river for awhile, and then the river veered right and disappeared until he had climbed higher, then it could be seen looking like a small creek moving along through a wooded area. He was up high and moving fast. He saw a sign that said ELKo-Two hundred and ten miles. Well, then it was Elko he was going to. He spent the night in Elko. He had gotten there in time to secure a room. He had come across the Hoover Dam on his journey-It was a sight to see! It's an amazing feat done by man (men) and an awesome feeling riding a Bike across THAT Grand Canyon!

Elko was not a big place but had a couple of casinos which wasn't one of his vices. He did decide to have his dinner in one of them, tho. They usually served reasonably good food and at a lesser price than some restaurants. Afterwards he stopped off at a local bar for a game or two of pool. There were two men, one about thirty-three and one around fifty, playing pool and one young man watching. When the older one beat the younger one, he said had enough for this time, so Mitchell stepped up and asked if the one there wanted to play a game with Him? They played five games—Mitchell won two of them. After the games, he went to his room and went to bed.

The next morning he arose early just before the sun arose . . . he was on his way, away from Elko when the sun came bursting over the hill of night and into Day! It was a beautiful, bright day! Mitchell was enjoying the ride. He soon came to a smaller road and he took it, after consulting his map, discovered that he could ride for about fifty mile on this road which intercepted back to Highway EIGHTY.

This road was very much a country road made for Bike riding! As he rounded a curve, there were many curves, he saw another small road leading from this one and he could see a creek off in the distance, so he turned onto it and rode on toward the creek. It was slowly moving past, but ran along beside the little road. It looked as if no one came this way very often. It narrowed some here and grass grew along its edges. The sun was shining on the water making it sparkle. Mitchell slowed his Bike and came to a stop and pulled to the roadside. He walked down to the edge of the creek and it was then he saw the body floating in the creek. It floated slowly past almost before he realized it was the body of a woman. There was a small piece of torn rope around one ankle. She looked to have been there for a couple of days at least. It brought back memories of Na. He didn't like to remember Vietnam! He'd spent six years there and if he concentrated he could see and SMELL it! Not all bad—the jungle was lush but the air was very muggy. He had been out most of the time—in the jungles. The Most Dangerous Animal was there—THE VIET Cong, vicious animal, no heart for any mankind, not even his own! They were everywhere—Up from the ground, up in the trees, in underground tunnels—always there waiting! He'd seen too many bad things that he'd tried to forget, but you don't ever forget, you just push them way down so far you can't see them anymore. He wouldn't wish Vietnam on even his worst enemy. It was a HELL-HOLE as far as he was concerned. He had spent almost thirty years trying to forget.

Suddenly he came out of his reverie and remembered the girl. She had already floated quite a way down farther. He started his Bike and rode slowly until he caught sight of her again. He needed to call the police—the Sheriff, someone. He took his phone and tried to call, but he couldn't get it to work—too far from anywhere. He didn't know what to do but just ride along and keep her in sight. The creek was running quite swiftly here for such a small creek, but he thought it might be part of a river, a smaller tributary. The road was narrowing and it became a trail. He knew he couldn't do anything but try again to call 911. His phone still was not picking up a signal. He had decided to turn around and go back to get someone to come get the body out of the creek! As he turned he thought he saw a man in the trees. Who would be way out here? so far from any place? He was just finishing his turn when out stepped a man with a 30-30 rifle pointed at Mitchell. "Who are you—and what are you doing here on private property?"

"I didn't know it was private property—there were no signs," said Mitchell.

"They've been torn down by trespassers—like you. What are you looking for?"

"I told you that I'm not looking for anything—I'm just our riding my BIKE. I saw the creek and came to look at it up close. It's really a nice big creek, isn't it?"

"It's really a tributary from the river," he said, "but it's a nice creek to live near."

"OH, do you live near here? I need to make a phone call—there's a body of a woman floating in the creek. Did you see her?" asked Mitchell. "We need to call the police, the Sheriff, or 911, somebody. My name is Mitchell Monroe and I'm on my way to Utah—Salt Lake and then on up to Wyoming." "Yes, I do live back down the trail a ways, come on—we'll make the call." Mitchell rode his bike, following the man back to his place. Soon a cabin appeared on a nice neat plot of ground. "Nice place," said Mitchell, "how long have you lived here?"

"Ever since I came back from Vietnam, I bought it then. I was married, but I guess the war messed me up for husband material—June left me the second year I was home. It's hard to get back to normal, isn't it—after Nam, I mean?"

"Yes, it is. We'd better make our call before it gets too late and they won't be able to remove the body before dark." Tyrone, as he said his name was, called the Sheriff who said he'd be out in a half hour at the earliest. Meanwhile, Tyrone and Mitchell went to see and the woman was still there, caught on a small branch in the water. They waited there for the sheriff who arrived in half-hour, and when the body was gone, Tyrone invited Mitchell to dinner at his place. Mitchell accepted The dinner of fried chicken, mashed potatoes, gravy and vegetables. There was even a pie.

"You bake pies?" asked Mitchell.

"No, I'm afraid not, a Mrs. Bradley in town bakes and sales them—you want coffee?"

"Sure," said Mitchell, "thanks for inviting me to dinner, Tyrone, I've enjoyed it." They ate their pie and drank their coffee. Tyrone asked, "Why don't you must spend the night here, Mitchell and leave in the morning? It's late now . . . maybe we can play a game of poker or dominoes before we retire for the night. There's a guest upstairs in the loft."

They were playing dominoes and Tyrone asked "How do you suppose she got in the creek?"

"Well, it could have happened in several different ways," said Mitchell, "she could have slipped in, or maybe went wading and the creek's flow was faster than she thought, she lost her footing—and maybe she didn't know how to swim?"

"Was she clothed or nude?" asked Tyrone.

"I thought maybe she got in to bathe and got caught on something that made her fall," said Tyrone.

"That's another possibility," said Mitchell. "Was she anyone you knew, Tyrone? a neighbor?"

"HA, as you can see, I don't have any near neighbors. The nearest one is about six miles West of here, the McClouds, and I know all of them. What did the Sheriff say? Was she old or young?" asked Tyrone.

"He really didn't say much," said Mitchell. "He did say that she wasn't any one that he recognized."

"You would think the local Sheriff would know just about everybody around and in his town or village, Wouldn't you? asked Tyrone. "Hey, maybe she floated from way up creek, miles away from here. How long did the Sheriff say she had been in the water?"

"Let's just drop the subject," said Mitchell—"I don't want to talk about or look at dead bodies. Just play dominoes, Okay?"

"Sure think," answered Tyrone, "didn't intend to upset your, Sorry!"

"It's not your fault, I just saw too damned many dead bodies back in Nam to last me a lifetime," said Mitchell. "Thanks for the dinner, the dominoes, and the offer of your guest room, but I'm going to hit the road. Thanks for your hospitality, Man"—Mitchell shook Tyrone's hand. He got on his Bike and left; Tyrone, the creek, and the memory of the body, behind, The moon came up big and bright and Mitchell rode on thinking good thoughts, enjoying the night ride, the feeling of freedom and the moonlight.

Moonlight always reminded him of Alexandra! They had spent many moonlight nights dancing till dawn, loving all day, and just sitting together holding hands and not even talking. This had lasted Eight months. He shipped out from the Philippines to Vietnam and she died five months later from a cancer she didn't even know she had. He had visited her grave on his way home after the war. Moonlight would always bring memories of Alexandra, his love.

He came to a place that looked like a good spot to sleep, to spend the night. It was off the road among some trees, just enough room for him and his Bike. He parked it in the ring of trees and took out his bedroll and spread it out. He lay down his gun within easy reach and fell instantly to sleep. He awoke sometime later, the moon was far into the west. What had awaken him? Voices! Men's voices talking. He put his gun in his hand and listened. They were talking about one of their girl. "She ought not to have done that. Jim knew she was messing around, You can always tell. "OH, He thought, just what I need—a bunch of drunks having girl trouble! At their next remark, Mitchell was wide awake! "but he didn't have to kill her. Someone will find her in the river, Stuck somewhere, the second voice said. "What if it took one of the tributaries and ends up in some small creek, stuck in driftwood. What if that happens?" this one asked. The next one made Mitchell's blood run cold. "OH, Hell, don't worry so much, it'll be months before she's found and the animals will have eaten most of her by then," this last voice said.

Mitchell could tell they were walking off to the East of him. He listened until he could hear them no more, pushed his Bike out to the road and rode out of there. He didn't stop until he had covered eighty miles and then only for fuel, a bathroom break, and a drink. He rode on for another hour before he stopped in a small place called Greatfeld and he stopped at their only cafe called The Hen House. It served breakfast all day long. He ate ham and eggs with hash browns and drank two tall cups of coffee. As he sat having his food, he wondered if the girl the man had killed was the one he found in the creek? He was glad he was far away from that area.

By evening he had reached Wendover just inside the Utah border. He stopped here for the night. He needed sleep! He slept for a while, woke up and couldn't go back to sleep. There was a bar across the street, so he walked across and entered. There were a few people still in there. Two men playing pool one just watching. Two others were playing cards at a table. He sat at the bar and ordered a beer. He was sitting there thinking that when he got to Salt Lake, he would look up the name, the real name of his father. His father had been adopted and didn't even know his Real name, but his adoptive mother on her death bed had told his father his real name—It was Spears. So Mitchell thought he'd do a little digging on the name.

All of a sudden, he felt eyes on his back. He slowly turned around to look—and there she sat! A very beautiful dark-haired girl with the most beautiful deep blue eyes he had Ever seen. She smiled at him "I see you couldn't sleep either. I saw you come in on your BIKE. I couldn't sleep so I came over for a drink." Mitchell picked up his beer and walked across to her table "Mind if I sit down?"

"Why, No, of course not. If I hadn't intended to sit and converse with you, would I have gotten up, dressed and walked across the street," she smiled at him.

"Maybe you just like Bikers," he said.

"I don't know any Bikers, you're the first one I've ever talked to. My name is Delish Whitmore, from Denver, Colorado."

"And what do you do in Denver?" asked Mitchell.

"OH, LOTS of things! I'm a librarian at a college there. I teach Ballet to Young girls, I ride in Rodeo parades on my palomino, and I take moonlight rides to relax my mind, body and soul. Anything else you'd like to know?"

"Do you belong to anyone—permanently, that is OR are you free to frolic with unmarried, older Bikers?"

"I am free to do *whatever* I *choose* to do, thing is, I Have Limits and Boundaries I've set for myself, to keep from becoming someone or something, I don't want to be."

"OH, A good head on your shoulders, I see. So, what do you say to coming to my room—perhaps we both can get some sleep," said Mitchell. She picked up her purse and held her hand out to him. He stood up, bought two more beers and took her hand they walked to his room. When they were inside, he opened the beer, sat on the side of the bed, patted it beside himself. She came and sat down beside him and he handed her a beer.

"From your speech, back in the bar, about your choices and boundaries—I take it you don't do this often?" asked Mitchell.

"Not at all! Never, but I told myself that at Forty-five, I can kick over the traces—BEFORE I become too old to kick them over! she laughed.

They sat and talked for several hours. He about his home life, his time in Vietnam—he even told her about Alexandra. She told him how sad it made her to hear this.

She told him She had been married once, long ago, when she was twenty. She loved this man dearly! But one day he came home, packed his things and left with no explanation. She found out later, that he had an affair with a woman a little older than himself and fell madly in love with her. In fact, they are still married as far as she knew, *BUT* once was enough for her—and she had never gotten an explanation from him. She felt for a long time that she wasn't woman enough to hold a man—but she met Bradley three years later and learned; That if she was women enough for Bradley, She was woman enough for ANY man. Her Bradley had died in a plane crash two years after she had met him. She was devastated But one can survive Great Tragedies! That was another lesson learned and filed in her heart.

They had talked so long that Mitchell had lain down with his head on the pillow and after a bit, still talking, she joined him. They both fell asleep playing there together.

The sun awoke them coming in thru a small window. Mitchell opened his eyes smiled into her big blue ones and took her in his arms. She came into them willingly and they were in bed for another hour—but—not sleeping! "Let's have some breakfast before we start farther on our journey, OK?" asked Mitchell.

"Lets," said Deliah, and they did!

She came out to get into her Mercedes and Mitchell had his BIKE ready to go. He walked over and put his arms around her, rocking her gently back and forth. "Thank You for a wonderful evening and night. I haven't talked so much since—I can't even remember when. I really enjoyed your company and companionship."

"Me too," said Deliah—"and IF you're ever in Denver—look me up—I'm in the phonebook. And thanks again for showing me your "BIKE," she said as she moved out, smiled and waved. He stood and watched her car until it was a small spot on the road.

Mitchell got on his bike and rode out of the town, out on the road. As he rolled along, he thought of Deliah who said he was the first Biker she had talked to. Maybe—and maybe not. It really didn't matter. She was a good conversationalist, and she wasn't a bad bed partner either. A girl who can make an old Biker's toes curl—is my kind of girl!

He rode on toward Salt Lake where he planned to do some sightseeing, and some checking on the Spears name. He should be there tomorrow sometime in the evening. He heard that the city was very pretty at nighttime. HE'd soon see for himself.

He arrived in Salt Lake around five O'clock P.M. the following evening, rented a room and then went for a ride to see part of the city—there was a lot of it!

Salt Lake is nestled in the ancient Bonneville Lake. He rode by to see the Tabernacle—a big place! He passed the International Headquarters of the Latter Day Saints. He was going to come back and check into the genealogy files for the name SPEARS. He would do that before he left here, maybe tomorrow Or the next day. He rode by the State Capitol Building. All capitol buildings he'd ever seen were beautiful, but this one ranked way high on the

"BEAUTIFUL" scale, and especially this time of evening—lights all it up. It really was a beautiful sight!

It was too late for sightseeing this evening, but tomorrow was another day. He wanted to go see the two homes of the Brigham Young families—the BEE HIVE and LION. Imagine one man with two houses of women and children! LUCKY and TIRED are the two words that came to his mind! Right now he was tired and hungry. He went into a nice looking restaurant and got a wonderful meal! Cooked to his liking and a very friendly waitress. He went to his room—Happy. There was a bar, not a big one. He passed its door as he went to the elevator. There was a piano playing Old songs and his feet, on their own, walked into the place, sat at the bar and ordered himself a beer. He was just relaxing and listening to the music when a youngish man of thirty-three or so who came to sit beside Mitchell and he stumbled and flopped himself on the stool bumping into Mitchell and spilling his beer. Mitchell calmly said "You owe me a beer, you just spilled mine."
"I'm not buying you a beer-you're big enough to take a little bump."
"You should have moved out of my way." Mitchell told the bartender to get him another beer and the young man would pay for it. Again the young man sneered that he didn't owe him a beer and wasn't going to pay for it. Mitchell was off the stool, his right arm across the young man's neck and his left arm high on his back where Mitchell had pushed it up. "You take your right hand, reach into your pocket and get the money for my beer." The young man was frightened anyone could see and he obeyed Mitchell's instructions. Mitchell released the young man and said "I don't mind being bumped accidentally—but an apology was all it would have taken. Now, I've taught you this lesson, gently—remember it well. Mitchell gave a pat to the young man's shoulder, picked up his beer and Thanked him, then walked to the elevator and up to his room. Why were these young men so up tight? he wondered and what happened to "I'M Sorry."

The next day Mitchell went to look up info on the Name SPEARS. He learned that they came from Scotland in the early Seventeen-hundreds. There were miners, farmers and carpenters, and scattered in between were two doctors, a veterinarian, a few teachers, etc. They settled in Georgia, Tennessee, Missouri, Alabama and one group to Virginia. The farthest back he could find for his father's group was Seventeen-Hundred and seventy-four. He was glad that he went and did some research on his father's REAL or biological name.

He did go by and visit the Bee Hive and the Lion houses which were nice homes for those days. Then he went to the Museum of Fine Arts. Now, that's an interesting place! Fascinating articles and paintings. He even went to see the Capital Theater—the Opera Company's Headquarters. Beautiful large and GRAND theater! Everything in Salt Lake was large—including the Great SALT LAKE, which the city was built near. Mitchell had been here for three days and had seen a lot. There were still two places he wanted to see before he left this area—the two forts; Fort Floyd and Fort Douglas. He did ride out and see both of them.

He was on the road again feeling excited and Happy! He had enjoyed his stay in Salt Lake, but he was happy to be on his way to Wyoming. He'd never been there, either. He was still on Highway Eighty.

The first town he hit right inside the state of Wyoming was Evanston, where he stopped to feed (FUEL) his (HOG) and himself. The cafe was about two blocks from where he'd *fueled* his Bike. It was a small Place but the food was good. HE wanted a beer with his steak, but he knew he couldn't ride off just after having a beer, so he settled for a glass of ice-tea, and was on the Bike again as soon as he swallowed his last drink. Highway Eighty thru this part of Wyoming went thru many small towns. He passed thru Fort Bridger and saw that there was a Historical Park and he took a side trip to see it. It was about like all Historical sites, some interesting information on things one never listens to in their History Class in Schools. From here he traveled to Rock Springs, a slightly larger town and then a little farther was Green River. He pushed on from Green River although it was late afternoon. He passed many SMALL towns until he came to Rawlins. He knew it was time to stop, so he began to look for a place to pull off and sleep for a while. He found a place that seemed okay. There was a tiny hill of rocks with a few trees, so, he rode his Bike out behind the hill, parked and got out his bedroll. He even took his tarp and put it over him, too. It was a bit cold right now. He lay down. He could hear the sounds of the night creatures which lulled him to sleep.

What had awaken him? He couldn't see anything and dared not move until his eyes adjusted to the darkness. He slowly, very slowly turned over and as he did, he glanced around and what he saw wasn't a happy sight, for there about thirty feet away sat three Bit, Grey, Wolves, in a row—watching him. Their eyes glowed red in the night's light. He knew there was no way of outrunning them, he wouldn't even reach his Bike. He slowly slide his gun into his hand, loaded it and shot into the air—they turned and walked away for a few steps, then turned his way again. The one who seemed to be the leader was daring! He kept inching toward Mitchell. He shot into the air again, and two of them went running off, but the brave one got ready to attack! He lunged for Mitchell and the gun barked again. It caught the wolf in the middle of his leap and the shot got him right in the heart. His momentum brought him to within a foot of Mitchell. Mitchell hadn't wanted to kill him. He was a handsome creature, but a vicious one. Look at those fangs! He had been caught in the middle of his SNARL and that was his DEATH MASK. Mitchell knew he'd better move on—he didn't want to be caught with a dead wolf and a gun in his hand. So, once more, Mitchell hastily put his things away and rode off into the early morning. His watch read Three-thirty A.M. He decided to ride on into Laramie before he stopped.

He reached Laramie about Seven A.M. He was TIRED as he hadn't slept enough and needed some sleep—but first—some coffee!—maybe breakfast? He pulled into a small place called "NELLIE'S BARN"—a very western looking place. Saddles, wagon wheel, harnesses and a few horseshoes on the wall. He sat down ordered coffee and steak and eggs. He was just relaxing when a newspaper caught his eye. "The body of a girl floating in a creek about two weeks ago has been identified and the killer has been apprehended. She was four months pregnant. The man who killed her was the baby's father. A young man who had been in trouble with the law since he was thirteen years old. A Tyrone Elliot Biggs had called the police when he and a friend, Mitchell found the body in the creek. The trial would begin on October the fourteenth, but it was reasonably possible though, that he would get life or?, because of the baby—a second life taken. Mitchell was glad they found him so quickly!

As he sat there thinking about his life, he thought of all his time in Nam. His dad had died of a brain tumor and his mother grieved herself into a home for Incompetent people. She had died last year—yet he could remember fishing with his father, icing homemade cookies for his mom. He remembered going on vacations to beaches, mountains and out to Yuma in the desert, one year to see his Mother's dad. He had lived in Yuma for many years. His mom lived there before she met his dad. Their meeting was rather a unique one! His dad had gone to look for work when he was young. He got stranded there in Yuma with no money (his old car had broken down) and no prospect of a job! He happened to stop one day at a Tire Place to see, if, perhaps, a mechanic there could look at his car. Mr. Aragon, the owner asked if he had a job? and when he answered No, Mr. Aragon said "I'll make a deal with you, I'll fix your car, if you will take my daughter to school each day. I can't do it and my wife doesn't drive.

"For how long do I have to do it?" asked my father.

"Well, this is her final year, and she only has four months to finish, is that too long?"

"But, I don't have any place to stay—to live—I would gladly do it to get my car fixed."

"You can sleep here in the loft, the room behind my Office. Until school is out and Enid is finished. You can help me some during the day while Enid is in school. DEAL?"

"Deal," said Dad, and they fell in love and got married the following year after Enid finished her schooling. When she got Huffy with him, Dad would say, "You're in my charge, Enid, I worked for you!" This always made her forget her anger. She would smile and come hug him, saying that she loved being in his charge. Mitchell smiled at the memory of dad telling him this story. Mitchell had hoped to find a woman like his mother, but the war came along and he was gone—for a long time. When he got back he visited his mother as often as he could, but she kept getting worse until she finally died. Mitchell was Ready for HAPPINESS—He had a good job, he owned a beautiful SEA Side cottage, a new car satin his garage at the house. He had made most of his money in Real Estate. He had written a book about his time in Vietnam and how he thought he was never coming home—and he didn't want to DIE—not THERE! and it sold Many copies, large and small.

When he got to Cheyenne, still on highway Eighty, he remembered that Deliah lived in Boulder, Colorado and he headed his Bike in that direction. When he got there he remembered her telling him that she was in the phonebook. She taught at a ballet school, so he called a few and found the one she worked for. "Did he want her to call Deliah to the phone? NO, he would see her after work, Thanks anyway."

He parked his Bike a block away and waited for her to exit the school. He saw her coming and his heart beat fast. He waited until she was even with the doorway where he had waited for her. He stepped out—and she came into his arms. It was pure MAGIC! and he said "I've wanted to see you again ever since I saw you drive away and your lights disappeared into darkness. I wanted to get on my Bike and overtake you—but I didn't want you to think *all* Bikers acted that way," he laughed. She was still inside his arms, she reached up and kissed him "I thought after the way I so easily went with you, as If I did that everyday, you would never want to see me again."

"OH, BUT I DO! I wanted to invite you down to visit me for a few days—I can take you on the Bike, but your car is a better idea for you, tho, How about it?"

"Yes, let's do that," she replied.

The following Monday found them in Miami, Florida. As she followed his Bike, in her car, she realized that they were in a very affluent neighborhood.

She supposed that he was showing her the RITZY part of town. When he pulled up and into the driveway of a large, elegant home (she had stopped at the curb) with palms, lush green lawns, she thought he was just showing her the house. He parked the Bike, came and opened her door and said "come on Deliah—Samson will show you his liar." She got out of the car and holding his hand, they walked up to the door and he unlocked it, stepped aside for her to enter. She looked at him Questionably. "Is this your idea of a Sea Side Cottage, Mitchell?"

"Yes, it is, Welcome."

"And I thought you were just an ordinary Biker. Do all Bikers live like this?"

"Only a few of us who get lucky," said Mitchell. "The only thing left to prove how lucky I am, really am, is to find me a lifetime mate."

"And what qualifications must she have to be eligible?" asked Deliah.

"Well, she must like Bikes—learn to ride behind the driver. She must be beautiful inside and out, a good conversationalist, a good judge of people. She must love me with all her heart, as I will love her—and she must NEVER cut my hair!" laughed Mitchell.

"Do you think you will ever find her?"

"I already have! One evening as I drank a beer in a small bar and she, never having talked to a Biker came to my room, slept in my bed without having sex (until morning). She is my kind of woman! I've loved her from that moment on."

"Do you believe she Never talked to a biker before?"

"Well it's okay either way—I'd never, just on a whim, taken a lady to my room and had no sex like that before."

"I guess we were made for each other. I must get my daring ways from my Great, Great Grandmother, EDWENA SPEARS who came over from Scotland in the SEVENTEEN-SEVENTIES. She was said to be a very unpredictable WOMAN.

"Why are you staring at me like that, Mitchell?—Did I say something wrong? Mitchell?—Mitchell?"

The End

D.B.

THE MISSING JEWELRY
OF
THE KING,' MISTRESSES, JEWELRY

DEDICATED TO MY SISTER-COUSIN

DELORIS ANN WILLIS

DELORIS GOES TO A YARD SALE AND AN ANTIQUE
SHOP WHILE IN A SMALL TOWN OF PROVINS, FRANCE,
FINDING AN UNUSUAL SET OF JEWELRY; ONE FOUND
FROM A YARD SALE AND ONE FOUND FROM THE
ANTIQUE SHOP—BUT THEY BELONG TO A TIME IN
HISTORY AND MUST BE RETURNED!

Deloris met her friends the night before she was leaving for France. They had dinner together at their favorite restaurant. After dessert, Deloris made her little speech saying; That she would miss all of them, terribly, but she needed a break and she wanted to go again to France, Paris to be exact. She had been there three years before and had later decided she would go there for an unlimited stay. She kissed them all goodbye, gave each a hug, told them she would miss them all—Alex most of all. He had been her strength at times—always there for her with a hug and a shoulder to cry on. She cried when she told him goodnight at the door. She told him that he was the only man she loved at this time, this made him laugh.

The next morning, 7 a.m., she was on her way. She had made a reservation at an Inn in Paris. She would later find herself a small place to rent. She might possibly buy later, if she decided to stay there.

One of the things she liked about Paris was the Later Nighters who sat at the outside cafes laughing, talking while they drank their wine, or tea. There were lovers too who walked arm in arm, stealing kisses every-one-in-a-while. Very Romantic thought Deloris. She felt relaxed and happier here among people who seemed to enjoy life in an easier and relaxed manner than the New Yorker's did.

She found a small place to rent the second week there. It was in the older part of the city. It was near enough for her to walk Square-Of-Time which had it's sidewalk cafes and Rues for strolling. Deloris loved on stroll and she wished she had someone to stroll with. This made her think of Alex which saddened her some. She wondered how he was doing?

Tonight she was on her way to see a play at a smaller theater a few blocks beyond the Rue Lavonne Square. She found her seat number and sat down to wait for the theater to fill. The play was rather a sad one. It was about a young couple who had trouble being together because of in-laws. He eventually realized he had to leave her, when he realized that the wife would never be free of per parents' control. It of course was dramatically done, as most plays were in Paris.

After the play she decided to stop for a glass of wine at one of the small cafes. She took a seat at a small table on the right enjoying her wine. She once again wondered what her friends Amanda and Michele were doing.

As she sat there thinking about her friends back in New York—in walked the actor of the play she had just seen. He smiled at her as he walked past to the table next to hers. "Am American!" he asked? When she glanced over at him she said, "Why, yes I am, and you're the man I just saw up on the stage of the theater, Aren't you?"

"Why, yes I am—how kind of you to notice. Did you like the play?" "Well, to be perfectly honest as we Americans are as I'm sure you have heard—I've seen worse and I've seen better. *HOW DID YOU LIKE IT?*" Deloris asked?

"I've also seen and DONE better, he said as he smiled at her. Have you seen enough plays, Yourself, to be a fair critic?"

"Well, I'm a drama major! I teach it!, but I don't know how "fair" I am, said Deloris Ann. How LONG HAVE *YOU DONE* DRAMA?"

"Oh, long enough to know a *good* lay from a bad one, but I'm not a young man anymore—I still have to eat, so sometimes I'll do a play that's not *too* good (the play, I mean) BUT I *AM A GREAT Actor*, he said laughing, which makes this play a little more successful—don't you think so?"

"Yes, I'm sure you are correct. Are you a True Parisian—or have you just *Rooted* here from some other place?"

OH! I'm a True Parisian, But I studied in your America—New York—when I was younger.

"That explains your acting ability," teased Deloris. I worked there for a few years, myself—doing some drama. I eventually moved upstate New York and opened my own Drama Academy. I'm here on vacation. I left my three best friends and instructors there. In fact, my friend Michele is from your country but she's been in America since she was ten years old. Her mother married an American Serviceman. Alex and the other one is a Drama Teacher. He's been with my school for about eight years and has been divorced for ten. Michele is single."

"ARE you married, he asked?"

"No, I'm Not, I was a long time ago for about four years, but not now." BY the way my name is Deloris Duncan she held out her hand.

"I'm Paul Travis Andrews," he said taking her hand. I'm so pleased to meet such a frank, straight-forward women" and his eyes held amused laughter.

"It's been a pleasure talking to you, Paul Andrews, when is the play due to close?"

"Next week is the last of this one but I'll be at the Florence Theater, on Rue Challis—It's a comedy—maybe you'll like it better?"

"I'll see what happens by then, and Thank You for your company this evening, I've enjoyed it. And with this Deloris walked out into the evening's soft breeze.

Deloris rented a car the next day and went SIGHT SEEING, into the smaller quaint towns and villages surrounding parts of PARIS. She took pictures of boats on a lake—beautiful big boats, blue skies. There were skiers on the lake, too and she took pictures of them.

Down in a small village she came upon a yard sale beside the road in front of a small cottage. She bought an old antique necklace—a thin gold chain with two tiny cherubs, one on each side. They were made of Platinum. On the bottom, hanging down from the chain, was a gold setting which held a larger angel, which opened to reveal a watch. It held what looked like a family crest. Each number place was a ruby. What an interesting piece! She paid more than she normally would have for a necklace BUT it was *very* different! She asked the seller if it was a family piece? The seller told her it had been in a box of jewelry that her husband's Great Aunt had left to him when she died. This piece was in a box that he hadn't even looked Thru but told her to sell it.

Deloris was Very Pleased with her purchase.

The following Wednesday found Deloris at the Florence Theater watching it fill and waiting for the show to begin. In a few short minutes the curtain went up and there on stage in bright red pajamas and house slippers, sat Paul Andrews! He wore a fake moustache, gray temples (they were his own). He was reading the Newspaper. In came his plump wife in a revealing, purple nightgown. She had bright red hair. She came to sit on his lap, but she missed somehow and fell on her bottom and she began to cry. He tried to lift her off the floor but couldn't. She kept slipping out of his grasp. He needed help, but her gown was so revealing he couldn't ask anyone to come help him get her up. As he pushed her on to her side—her large breast came partially out and he quickly but her on her back. Then the slit on her nightgown exposed her black, lacy panties with their red bow. He tried again to lift her, this time one breast came ALMOST completely Out as her gown came up to her waist, showing the back of her panties—and—there wasn't a back to her panties. The audience was roaring in laughter at this point—and the curtain fell.

Deloris decided that the comedy was more to her liking than the Drama had been. Mr. Andrews was as good in comedy, perhaps better, than he had been in his Drama. Of course, every actor knows that comedy was harder to Pull Off than just about any other kind of acting. People who have done both say this. She walked home smiling.

The following evening she was sitting outside one of the cafes, having a cup of tea, listening to conversations nearby and watching the Strollers, When down the street HE was coming in her direction. As he came near and noticed her, he smiled and asked "may I join you?" as he seated himself. "Lovely evening for a Stroll—care to accompany me?"

Deloris looked at him and thought WHY NOT? As they strolled he asked "Did you happen to see the play at the Florence, and if so, how did you like it?"

"I went on Wednesday last and I enjoyed it very much!" said Deloris, you do comedy well. Do you prefer comedy?"

"Actually said Paul, I just love being on stage!—Drama or comedy, but I must admit—I *do* love a *good* comedy!"

They walked along comfortably and quietly for a little while. He suddenly asked "Do you miss being married?" I wonder why I haven't gotten married again? I would like to have had children, before I become This old. Do you have children?"

"OH, NO, I, too have waited too long and I've never found a man I wanted to marry again after bob. I was always too busy for romance—isn't that an awful thing to say?, but it's true." I always had my Drama Academy, always teaching my students. "No time for romance. What did you do before acting—did your parents approve of you being a actor?"

"They always supported me in any choice I made, said Paul, they were great Parents. I first became a lawyer, studied for it in collect and after a time, studying law—I became aware that being a lawyer no longer made me happy. One summer on my vacation I did some summer stock and I was Smitten by the acting bug. I gave up being a lawyer and began acting. My parents eventually came to terms with it. They were killed in an auto accident two years into my being an actor. I felt guilty for awhile, but my therapist set me straight on how parents love their children—no matter what they do—the career. After this understanding, I began to enjoy my acting—without guilt, and here I am fifty still upon the stage!"

They had stopped for a minute and Deloris said, "I'd better get back now. I've rented a car to drive to the small town of Provins tomorrow and look around. I hear it's a friendly little place. There's a small antique Shop there I was told that sells nice, old antique jewelry." She said this as they were strolling back to the square. When they reached it Deloris said, Goodnight and Thanked him for the stroll. He asked if he should walk her to her place but she told him she would be fine and again she said, Goodnight.

She slept soundly and awoke early had her coffee and croissant, the picked up her car and drove to Provins. It was a lovely day and she was enjoying her drive, when all-of-a-sudden she realized she had taken a wrong turn. The town was nowhere in sight! She stopped and took out her map and saw where she had erred, so she turned around and drove until she saw where she should have turned right. The sign told her she had 3 more miles till she reached Provins.

She loved Provins at first sight! There were flowers everywhere; on walls and in every planter in sight. In the Center, it had a park with a central stage. "What a lovely place to perform Skits for the town's people;" thought Deloris. She drove on to find the Antique Store and there it was; right next door to a country store. She parked her car and went into the Antique Shop. The woman behind the counter said "Welcome—if you need help—just call me," and she went back to reading her book. Deloris saw many cute things and she had just walked up to the second counter which held Old Antique Jewelry. In the lower shelf of the case her eye caught something familiar; Was that a brooch and earrings with Cherubs? Why they seemed to be a part of the set that matched the necklace she had purchased at the Yard Sale last week. Yes, they were just like her necklace! The brooch looked as if it opened. She called the woman over and asked her to open the case. She told her she wanted to see the brooch, was so excited about her TREASURE. As she left the shop she saw that the stage was being used—someone was doing a Skit.

As she drove around looking the area over, she realized again she had taken a wrong turn. She was on a lovely country lane with wild flowers and trees in bloom. She had driven about a mile when she discovered that she was on a dead end street. She stopped at the wire fence-gate that was pushed shut. By looking closely she could see a small cottage back thirty yards or so, sitting among trees and flowery vines. She wanted to see it up close. She got out of the car walked to the gate to see if it was locked. That's when she saw the FOR SALE sign laying on the ground about ten feet inside the fence. She slowly—pushed the gate open, and leaving it Wide Open, she walked toward the cottage.

It was a charming old place she could see, not a big place but still a Sound Structure. It had been painted, light, buttery yellow. There were white shutters on the front windows. Deloris walked around back and found a brick patio surrounded by vines with purple blooms running across the small fenced backyard. There was another structure farther back. It wasn't exactly a barn but some kind of a tack room.

Some old reins and a skeletal saddle. It was dusty cobwebby, but also a Sound Structure. There was a well-house with a hand pump but all hooked to electricity. As she went back to her car, she took the number of the real estate from the sign. She tucked it in her purse intending to call later. It would make a lovely Country Place!

She stopped a few more places, had lunch and drove back to Paris. She dropped off her photos to be developed, the ones she had taken on her drive around and through the Town of Provins. There was one of the little Cottage!

That evening she sat outside a small cafe thinking about the cottage, deciding to make her call for information on it—tomorrow. First she must go over her Financial holdings. To see which way she would have to go to purchase it—and IF she planned to live in France for awhile. This thought led to How she could make her way Financially here in France. She could always get a job teaching Drama—If there was a need of one—Where?—Paris?, surely not in Provins?—Well, maybe! She had seen a Drama in the central square. No, she'd probably have to work in Paris. There would be some driving to be done if she lived in Provins and worked in Paris. Could she do that? Maybe—IF she worked for three days a week and IF she could get a job with the Provins Drama for the two days a week—she was sure she could manage. After all she still had the monies from her divorce settlement from Bob and a smaller one from her parents, and from the sale of the Drama Academy. So the next day she called and made arrangements to go back to Provins on Saturday, meet the broker and look the property over with the eagle eye of a buyer.

Saturday she was up early and ready to go see the cottage. She drove down early to Provins and had her breakfast in the small cafe there. When she finished her breakfast she drove out tot he cottage. It sat at the End of Rue le Fluer. She arrived there a few minutes before the realtor. When the realtor arrived she parked her car behind Deloris' . . . . got out, met Deloris at her car and introduced herself as Melanie McGarth. She unlocked the front door then stepped aside for Deloris to enter. Deloris was immediately enchanted with what she saw. There were windows all along the right wall of the living room. The ceiling was a bit lower than most houses of later dates. It was very quaint! It had a fireplace with a wooden mantel with a large mirror above it. It had its original wooden floor. On either side of the fireplace were bookshelves, with arch shaped tops. The fireplace was on the far end of the living room. "The kitchen must be behind the living room," thought Deloris. There were two windows on the opposite side of the living room—on the East. Vines growing on a trellis could be seen thru these windows. There was a door into the kitchen on the fireplace wall, to the left side of the bookcase. It was a County Kitchen with a floor of light green tile. Still quite shiny after all these yeas. NO, it has been retiled a few months ago. It had a wall of cabinets with cupboards above along the right side of the room which housed the stove and refrigerator. There were more of the same cabinet/cupboard along the back wall where the sink was placed a window above. A door to the Patio was just past the end of the sink wall of cabinets. A corner shelf stood in the left corner near the back door. On the left wall of the kitchen was a wooden server, built into the wall. The table and chairs were placed in the center of the room.

Past the server was a door on the left wall was a bedroom. The back wall that you faced when the door was opened, was of beadboard, all white. On closer inspection Deloris could see that there were double door sin the beadboard wall. They were hard to distinguish as they were cut from the all itself. When these were opened by Melanie, the room was a sunroom with windows on the three sides. It could be used as another bedroom because it had shades on all three sides to close out the sun and light. Deloris thought this was a very romantic and useful extra room.

Deloris knew she loved the place and she knew she would and could buy it. But she wanted to talk to Alex first. She told the realtor to let her think it over and she would let her know on Saturday, but she was somewhat sure she would purchase it. She just had to speak to Alex first.

When she called to speak to Alex he wasn't home so she called Amanda, Michele answered telling her that Amanda and Alex had gone off together for the weekend to Maine. She told Michele that she would call later. Tell both of them that she misses them.

She was so absorbed in thought that it took a minutes to realize someone was standing beside her table. She looked up and there stood THAT actor, Paul Travis Andrews and he asked "Where were you—lost in thoughts—so deep? May I sit?"

"Yes, please do. I was just thinking about a place down in Provins that I saw last weekend, and I'm thinking of either renting or buying it! It's a lovely Country cottage about a quarter of a mile off the main Road, at the end of Rue le Fleuer. It's older and has character. How would you like to see it? and give me your opinion?"

"Are you serious?" he asked. I'll give you an opinion of the house, but since I know nothing of your finances—or plans, I can only opine on the house itself. Is that alright?"

"Sure," said Deloris. I'm going down on Saturday, can you come with me then?"

"I can," said Paul. "What time and where?"

"Just meet me about eight a.m. on Saturday—I have rented a car."

Saturday morning found them driving to Provins. Just before they got to the turn for town, Deloris turned off on Rue le Fluer. She stopped at the gate. "This is it," she said, "isn't it a lovely place? I love all the flowers, plants and vines—such colors!"

"Well, I must say—it's a Charmer! Look at that Chimney." There atop sat a big crow looking quite content. "I wonder if he's a permanent resident? Maybe he lives in your Tack Room? You did say you had a Tack room?"

It was at this moment that the realtor drove up. "Good Morning," she said, "I see you've brought your friend today."

"Yes," said Deloris. Melanie McGarth, meet Paul Andrews. They shook hands.

Deloris was watching to see what reaction she got from Paul, upon seeing the inside. As the door was opened and he entered, his expression was surprise and happy at what he saw. "Lots of nice windows—AND a fireplace?" He quietly said to Deloris as they exited the living room. His eyes lit up again when he saw the kitchen.—But the biggest Surprise was the bedroom's back wall that revealed the other bedroom or Sunroom. On the left wall of the Sunroom, which Deloris hadn't noticed, was a door that opened onto a wooden porch that filled that whole corner of the yard. Next they saw the Tack room and the well-house. The well-house still had its room above it. There was an outside stairway that went up to the room over the well-house. It still held an old rocker, a small table, and an old cot. It had a small oil heater in the corner. Deloris assumed that a caretaker had *bunked* here. When they had seen everything and were at the car, Deloris told Melanie she would meet her on Wednesday morning to SEAL THE DEAL! They shook hands and left.

"Well," asked Deloris, What do you think of the cottage?"

"It is a beautiful little place—but it has its pros and cons: It REALLY is off the Beaten Track and quite a drive everyday to Paris—If one commuted—but on this other hand, look at the amazing scenery of color! Another Pro is that the woods are away from the back of the property for a few hundred feet so no one could sneak up on you. Now for a con—it is quite a distance to go for groceries—more commuting. ALL in ALL, I think it's a beautiful place to live!—could be a little lonely—but? *IF* I wanted it—*I'd* buy it in a minute—and IF I were financially able to afford it. THOSE are MY thoughts in a NUTSHELL."

"I'm going to buy it," she stated. "Do you thin it possible if someone wanted too—to make a Dance School or perhaps a theater from the old Tack room? Maybe even a Drama school?"

He looked directly into her eyes and said "I think that would be a damned good idea.—Or—a Bed and Breakfast Inn.

Deloris checked on positions for work in some of the Drama Schools. After looking for almost a week—she found one that she thought was best for her. She could work four days a week which left her with a three day weekend. She told the owner of the school that she would let her know for sure on the following Friday if she was interested in the position.

On Wednesday she sealed the deal for her cottage. She was so excited to be its owner! The more she studied the Tackle Room and Bunk house, she could see that a Bed and Breakfast was a feasible objective. Maybe, somehow she could connect it to the well House room. She liked the idea, or make a smaller suite around the well house for A HONEYMOONERS suite? Yes, she was going to see exactly, what she could do with the WELL HOUSE!

She finally connected with Alex telling him about her cottage and her job offer at a Drama School. He told her that he would be over for a visit during the Christmas Holiday to see her place, and to hold off on the job for now and concentrate on her cottage. He'd be arriving on December eighteenth and did he need to make reservations? Or would her cottage be available?

You need no reservations, Alex, I have my *own* Cottage!

She took Alex's advice and went to work putting things into HER cottage. She bought furniture for the living room; two loveseats, two over-stuffed chairs that she found at an antique Shop. A large table-desk, a floor lamp, two lamp tables. She purchased draperies for the row of windows in the living room and on the two windows on the East Wall. She also purchased two occasional tables, A bamboo chair and coffee table. It was a comfy room! She would use the gas fireplace when the weather got colder.

For the kitchen she purchased a square table and six chairs, also curtains and a tablecloth, even a tea set for the top of the server.

For the bedroom she bought; a Sleigh Bed, a bedside round table for a lamp, a pole lamp, a double chest of drawers, a tall, narrow bookcase and a rocker.

For the Sun-Room-bedroom; An old Metal bed from an antique place. It had a colorful scroll panel in the center of the headboard, and the footboard. She put a square metal table with green metal leaves to hold the lamp. At the end of the bed she placed a teakwood trunk. A dresser with double rows of drawers. In the right hand corner of the room was the bathroom—with a door that opened inward that accessed the main bedroom. The window in the bathroom was left uncovered. This was as ready as Deloris wanted the house to be. Paul Andrews had come down one Saturday and trimmed the shrubs, plants and low trees by the Patio. He brought a friend who built a small courtyard of stone and a flowerbed surrounding it. She had bought a birdbath for this area and two benches. She hired a man to come and take the wire fence down and put a white picket fence across the front of the property.

The more she thought about her prospect of a Bed and Breakfast inn, she thought it was a good, even Great Idea!

She just plain relaxed and was enjoying her Summer. She went to a few more of Paul Travis' plays. She decided that she liked his comedy Best. He had come down a couple of times and spent Saturdays there with her. They went antiquing and once to watch the young Drama Group perform their Skit. And one beautiful Summer day, they drove over to see Fontainebleau Chateau. It had beautiful formal gardens and grounds around the Chateau, and marvelous art, carpets, tapestries on the walls and Very Grand stairways! In one word—Awesome! They enjoyed their visit there very much, She and Paul enjoyed each other's company more than she thought they ever would. He was fast becoming a major part of her life.

One day Deloris decided that she would go up into the Well-house and clean it—maybe put a rug down and new bedding for the cot. Clean and polish the table lamp, take a new pad for the rocker. Once up there, she discovered a small closed-like place and realized it had been the "Water Closet" (bathroom) and there was water and a Chamber-Pot. The little room had been papered in Old newspaper, many layers of paper. She began to peel the layers off and putting it in a pile on the floor. She had pulled off many layers and as she went to pick up the pile and move it out of her way, the whole pile toppled over and as they scattered something caught her eye. There was a piece laying there amid this mess that caught her attention was a picture of? of?—Her Angel Cherub necklace and earring set—and Even the Brooch! She took the section, carefully from among the mess and spread it out to read what it said. The date on the newspaper was Oct. nineteen-thirty-nine. The article stated that these were stolen jewels, stolen or lost? during the war—perhaps lost in travel, a transfer from one place to another during night time travel and carried by couriers who were found dead and the jewelry which had been given to one of the "KINGS OF OLD" Mistress, had been taken. It had been on its way to the Museum when it disappeared one night. It was priceless—made of gold and had platinum cherubs and ruby insets for numbers and embellishments. The set consisted of: necklace, earrings, brooch and a ruby and platinum ring. A great reward had been offered for its return. Deloris stood there in Shock! Could these be—or were-they her antique jewelry? from her country yard sale? She had bought them at separate times and places. But both places were here in Provins. Were there people still looking for them? She was sure that she had the jewelry in her possession right now! Not the ring. Where was it?

She had intended to take them and place them in a Safety Deposit box at the Bank. But now she wasn't sure that was a safe thing to do. What if someone saw what she had and asked questions? These were the treasures that belonged to a Country—their Museum of Royal Treasures. Who had stolen them and lost them—somehow? OR found out how priceless they were and hid them away? Deloris was trying to remember what the old lady said-the one she bought them from. She had said that they were left to her husband by an old Great Aunt when she died, and he hadn't even looked to see what had been in the box. Did he know but didn't want to be connected to them?

Deloris decided then and there to Never show her TREASURES to anyone! not anyone!—BUT she'd keep her eyes open for that

little houses' yard sales. Maybe the ring was there in another
unopened box.

After this discovery, Deloris put the old newspaper in the attic.
Then she finished revamping the Well-House room.

For the next few days her mind was busy working on what to
do with the jewelry? She Wouldn't DARE to wear any of the pieces.
Anyone who had been around in Nineteen-thirty-nine would or
might see it and remember and connect it to the news story, OR
think that someone in her past family had been connected to its
disappearance. She had put the old newspaper with the story away
in the attic, in an old trunk. She thought she would show it to Alex
when he got here at Christmas time. See if he had any suggestions.
Meanwhile she finished the Well-House room. She had a building
company come out and build a balcony on three sides and a wider
porch on the front. There was room on the wide front porch of the
well room for a small table and two chairs and a longer bench. She
loved the way it looked! Next she had a company come and put a
bathroom (sink, commode, corner shower) in the WATER CLOSET.
She painted the rocker a dark barn red and put a floral pad with
celery green, butter yellow rose and blue. The three windows, one
on each side of the back, had stripes in the same colors as the floral
in the pad. A new cover for the cot in a wide stripe of red, blue and
yellow. There was a new wooden floor in the bathroom and Deloris
put a rug there with towels to match. The new Patio deck on the
front of the Well House was entered from a French door. It wore a
thinner curtain that matched the others in the room. The deck was
on the East side, perfect for having coffee there in the mornings. She
had a new outside stairway built, too. It had a small landing about
one-third of the way and a thin tree sat there in a planter. The well
house would make a wonderful guest house even IF the Bread and
breakfast Inn never happened. Deloris was so very happy with her
home. She had a trellis built over the entry to the yard and her Patio.
She had planted pink climbing roses to trail over the trellis as they
grew. She hugged herself with happiness every time she drove down
Rue le Fluer to Her house!

One Saturday she decided to go out behind to the back part of her property and see what it was like. There was a small vineyard, only ten rows—short rows just past the three apple trees, on out to a creek that ran through her property. Way out in the right hand corner, pretty much covered with vines full of jasmine, was an old outhouse. She pulled away some of the vines and opened the door watching out for spiders and scorpions. In the corner of the outhouse were a stack of newspapers, old newspapers. She removed the plastic covering them, she pulled one off, then two, three and the fourth one had an item on the missing jewelry. This account stated that all the missing treasures of the Kings were returned—but the necklace, earrings, and brooch and the ring. It was believed that possibly one of the couriers had escaped being killed and had somehow stolen these items during the transferring from one place to another. ALL the couriers had been killed and none of the items had ever shown up. They just disappeared. The Only Other Person who MIGHT have stolen them would have been the driver of the truck, BUT he had died a few months later after the treasures were returned or found, EXCEPT the King's mistress' jewelry.

Deloris was at a loss as to who could have had them before she came upon them in the antique shop and at the yard sale at that little white house on the edge of Provins. She decided to see if she could discover <u>if</u> the antique dealer knew the old lady who lived in the little house.

The next day Deloris drove to the Antique Shop. She browsed for awhile and then she took her earrings out and showed them to the dealer and asked "have you ever seen a ring to match these?" The dealers aid "No, that she had bought these ones at a yard sale out on the edge of Provins, a little out in the country, not too far from here. Deloris asked for directions to where she had gone to the yard sale. She found the house. She walked up to the door. A smallish woman whom she recognized as the one who had sold her the necklace. Deloris explained that she had bought a necklace from her a couple of months ago. It was found in a box of jewelry that you said was left to your husband by and old Great Aunt. I am looking for a ring

Errors, Encounters and Escapades

that matched it. The old woman asked "Who told you to see me about this?"

Well, Deloris said, I bought a brooch from the antique Store in Provins and I asked her where had she gotten it? and she said she had gotten it from you sometime last year.

"Why is this so important to you? the little lady asked?"

"Oh, It's just that she thought she had seen a ring that matched the brooch in your box of the inherited things of your husbands. I just wanted to purchase it because it matched OR, looks similar to my brooch."

"OH, well, I don't know if there's a ring or not. You can look thru it if you want to."

"That would be Great," said Deloris. They both sat down to look when it was brought into the room. "What a nice Old Great Aunt to leave all of her jewelry to her Great nephew! Did she live near here?"

"NO, she lived in England all her life, but she vacationed here each year with my husband's grandmother—they were sisters. Her husband worked for the government when they were young. In fact, her husband was a courier for the Royal Museum during and before the war in the late part of the years, nineteen thirty eight and thirty nine. His job was to get the art and antiques out of the city and to a safe place. She was always Proud of him. He was a tall handsome man and always appeared to be so much in love with her. She was devastated when he died. She became very ill some months after he died and she died about a year later. That's when my husband found out that she had left everything to him. He never even looked thru the things. He sold a lot of them to antique places and the rest, this box, he gave to me for my yard sales," she finished.

"What an interesting story," said Deloris, "rather romantic." "Here, Dear, look thru this while I make us a cup of tea, alright?" "That would be nice," said Deloris, "Thank you!" she looked and looked again but no ring could be found. Maybe the handsome Uncle know of another who loved rings and one favor deserves another thought Deloris—maybe someone bought it years ago.

The lady Mrs. Adams as she had introduced herself, brought in the tea and as she sat down, she suddenly straightened up and said, "I think she was buried in that ring. I remember my husband's Grandmother saying that there was a special ring to be laced on her finger before she was buried. It was a *special* ring her husband had given her and it was not to be worn out in public, only with him in private. In fact, I believe I have a picture of her wearing it. *It* was o*n* her fi*n*ger, Mrs. Adams left the room and returned in a few minutes and held out a picture to Deloris. There lay a lovely Old Lady, laying peacefully in her repose, hands clasped on her stomach—and there on her finger was the ruby and angel ring!

Deloris thanked her for her time and information about the ring and the story of a long ago courier who took beautiful, beautiful pieces a Set of jewelry for his MOST Loved Lady. Now Deloris knew Who had taken the missing jewelry of a King's mistress. Somehow she didn't feel so bad about the missing ring—she knew it would never be found BUT, her pieces must be returned to their rightful place, *But* she wanted to talk to Alex first.

He came for the Christmas Holiday. They had such a good time together, just like old times. He was still her only love—But Paul Travis Andrews was a very close runner-up!—who would, in time, win her heart.

Deloris DID have a Bed AND Breakfast INN made from her Tack room, her bunk house and her Well House, which was one of the favorite rooms of all her rooms and suites.

She did call the Royal Museum, telling them that she had items of Great interest to them. They came and many questions were asked and the jewelry was taken. A few weeks later she was notified of a large amount of monies to be transferred to her bank as a reward for returning the treasure to the Royal Museum. It was enough to pay the cost of the building of her Bed and Breakfast! It was a successful venture her place was very busy and filled all Summer vacations and some in the off SEASON.

The Off season was the time her friends usually came to visit. They even did some acting while they were there for Deloris and her New Man—Paul Travis Andrews who would always be an actor, who entertained her—on stage and Off!

In looking back—Deloris was so glad she had sold her academy and come to France! She was a lucky lady—to have her dream of living in France come true and to find someone who loved acting as much as she did, and yet loved Her more even than acting. Yes, she was a lucky Lady even without the "Mistress' Jewels, She felt Wealthy in Love!

Biography

I was born in Fox Oklahoma on DECEMBER thirteenth, Nineteen Thirty-Five. I started school there and went on through the fifth grade. The family then moved to Manitou, Oklahoma, another little "One-Horse Town" as anyone who has lived in one—will know what I mean by this remark! BUT, let me say right here; that I liked living there, going through Middle School. THAT's where I met Coach Little—the basketball coach that I had thru HIGH School. HE Was a wonderful man and a darn good coach! Our Basket Ball Team went almost to STATE ONE YEAR,, We lost the last game before by two points! I went to FREDERICK HIGH School, but left before graduation from there.

IN my lifetime I'VE done lots of things—workwise. During the summer school break, I, LIKE LOTS OF TEEN, CHOPped cotten, pulled boles (cotten) and thanks to an Uncle who was a farmer—I learned to milk cows and how much work a farm demanded. I learned that hard work brings prosperity!

Later as a young woman I worked in a small Italian cafe, located near a large college, so it was a busy little place! I waited tables, made coffee (We caught all the truck drivers (FED.X, And U.P.S) to name a few and then I washed the dishes @WE had some college clientale, too.

By this time I had been in California for awhile. It was about this time that I met my soul mate, home on leave from the navy. HE returned in two years and we were married. We have four children. when my last child started Kindergarten I went to work as a classroom aide for the Campbell, C.A Elementary School

DISTRICT. I=worked there for seventeen years. I met many wonderful people there! I worked with well trained teachers—male and female.

I was President of our (THE AIDES) Chapter of California School Elementary Assoc., FOR TWO: MAYBE THREE years. I was always an active member before and after I was PRESIDENT!

When my father became fatally ill with cancer, I came to FRESNO C.A to care for him until he left for his heavenly journey. I had become attached to Fresno and we decided to move here. We've enjoyed this venture!

I BEgan to write and finally published one of my books! Since this I'VE published another one and the third one is, at this moment, being published! MY soul mate refuses to retire completely and still works a few hours a day.

I never intended to become a writer, but the words and phrases kept coming into my brain, quietly, on little cat feet, and once I began to hear them—I began writing them down on paper-and one word led to another, and another until I had a BOOK!!

SO, I see my writing as a gift from above, as are MANY THINGS in my life!

I was raised with lots of love from my parents. I married my soul mate and I HAVE FIVE WONDERFUL children, eleven grandchildren and ten great-grand children!

I consider myself a very Blessed Person!!